for my best friend:
loneliness

About the author:

Martin Wolkner, born in the metropolitan area Ruhr in 1980, studied English and German Linguistics, Film Studies and a little bit of Philosophy at Ruhr-Universität Bochum and University of Hull.

He worked as a writer, journalist, film critic, translator, subtitler and director of Filmfest homochrom in Cologne and Dortmund.

He has published two German novels and a collection of German poems. An English collection of poetry will follow soon.

The novella "Where Clouds End" was written between October 1999 and the summer of 2000. After extensive revision it was first published in 2019 in English and German.

Where Clouds End
The Story of a Dark Soul

A Novella by
Martin Wolkner

Bibliographical information of the German National Library:
This publication is registered in the German National Bibliography
at Deutsche Nationalbibliothek; detailed bibliographical data
is available on the internet via http://dnb.dnb.de.

Production and Publishing:
BoD – Books on Demand, Norderstedt

ISBN: 9783749465965

CONTENTS

*"I long
for feelings
as deep as
the ocean,
comfort,
closeness,
warmth,
protection,
love."*

*"I'd like to feel my body
and the motions of my heart,*

yet I don't feel any of that…"

1

He was almost out of this world. Although he still lingered on in it, there were hardly any hints that he was there, because he kept himself away, as far away as he could, from all life. The pain alone was with him. How satisfying solitude can be! What pleasure it is, if one must deny oneself everything else! What liberation, if one feels lost in life, lost in the fortune of the world!

It was still there with him and it did not want to dissolve, this pain, however much he endeavoured. The bittersweet pain was always present, and his strength was banned to that dark and secret place and concealed there, along with his feelings and memories. He was living a shadow life. He had become estranged from the light and he could not fight any more. For him there existed no past, no present, no future anymore, only pain. And to this he clung, for it was the only thing that was left to him. It confirmed again and again that he was doing the right thing. For if some day it was not there anymore, then indeed he had done something wrong and broken all his values and intentions.

But those long years of habituation had not deadened him. For that, he was much too cautious. When for the first time he had felt this bitterness, this melancholy, which had descended upon him like a black shroud, was unimportant, because that's the way things were and the beginning forgotten, like so much else from his lost childhood. Apart from the tiny spark of blitheness at his very beginning, he remembered only the heartache and he was probably even born with it. His constant companion was something valuable and essential to him, without which he would not have wanted to live on; a travelling companion that had become so vital that one followed them at the next fork of the road and made their path one's own. The pain was the only thing that there was no doubt about.

He sat in the branches of his friend, the lonesome oak, which stood on top of a gentle hill in the middle of a vast meadow. The seldom trodden path with speckles of coarse pebbles ran across the mound a stone's throw away from the oak. The hillock arose from the ocean of forests all around at the foot of it like a grass covered isle.

He sat in the crown of the tree and overlooked the landscape dominated by broadleaf forests and meadows. Somewhere almost at the horizon, the swathe of a wide motorway meandered through the countryside and destroyed the beautiful view, just as the dozen of power lines did which swung from pylon to pylon and which gave indirect evidence that possibly he was not alone in this sea.

Certainly, September had had its merits, sunny and warm, but now it was late October. The trees had turned the colour of their leaves already, early according to season, were crimson, almost purple, and had almost completely been deprived of their leaves by the storms that had raged. Even now a cool breeze was blowing through the boughs and twigs of his friend, which was strong and hardy. Its leaves had turned, but, in contrast to the others', they were still fiery red and dense. Yet it would not last much longer. Soon everything would be bare and dreary and grey like the sky, over which a thick carpet of clouds chased along. His gaze wandered over this carpet, as if he went over it for a walk. The majority of people did not like such weather; it dampened their spirits and souls. That was one of the reasons that hardly anybody went past this place. In principle, humans rarely came walking through the forest and over this meadow. This place was peaceful, calm, calming. Lost in thoughts he did not at all notice that the wind grew gradually stronger and colder, nor that it was piping a gruesome melody of farewell on the twigs of the oak. For a short moment he became aware of the wind sneaking in through his clothes and pinching his warmth. Not even this was left for him, the last bits of that which he really longed for, if he had but admitted it to himself. The more he fought against his yearning for warmth, closeness and company, the stronger it was smouldering subliminally for fulfilment. For the blink of an eye this desire sparked up again, fanned by the cold October wind, and he used all his rationality against it. That the world was bleak and cold he was convinced of, and he could experience it himself again and again, just like in this moment. In this, as in any other respect, nobody was able to fool him. He had gone through enough to know the world. There had been enough disappointment after disappointment in his life, enough humans who had abused him or deceived him or left him. Then he forgot about the yearning again.

The view on the valley was breathtaking. The blended surface of treetops below him, which were shaken to and fro by the wind, reminded him once again of the vast sea, which swells and surges and moves incessantly. The last shreds of foliage were being torn from the trees like rags of a beggar and swirled through the air like dandelion clock seeds in summer. The wind turned swiftly and swept his prey, the leaves, towards him and his friend, and veiled them in a cloud. Filled with enthusiasm for this spectacle of nature, he realised that nature was the only one allowed to give him true pleasures. Those of the world of man were untouchable for him, if he did not want to betray himself. Humans were only cruel; nature alone was beautiful in her cruelty. Even now she demonstrated this side of her, and he cherished it greatly that the leaves swirled around him sitting in the protection of the oak tree, and to know that this joyful pastime was the prelude to the rigor mortis of winter.

Slowly the clouds were darkening, while the veiled sun approached the horizon. Soon it would go down and leave the world shrouded in nightly blue shadows. For this reason it was about time that he took his leave and set out for home. Yet there was still some time left, a little bit of time which he wanted to use. In the duty of gloominess, a strong unexpected feeling of longing and sadness took hold of him. He felt the tickling in his nose and the gentle welling-up of tears in his eyes. There was a motion in him, a yearning for someone to whom he was connected, a craving for a strong friendship, understanding and sincerity, which he did not want to notice, because it was impossible for him to gratify its gravity. There was no human being who was willing or able to get involved with him in the way he was in need of, and there was no permission on his part to get engaged in any kind.

Within he heard the lamenting, stately music of a flute accompanied by a guitar, the music of his sadness resounding in his mind. It blended with the piping and whispering of the wind, which drowned out his quiet sobbing and carried it away, away from the oak over the open meadow. Tears were running down his face while he was wondering from which corner of his heart this hint had come and what it meant. The chill of the air made him sense the paths of the paindrops markedly on his face. His heart was open and at the same time empty yet full. It happened quite frequently that he felt like this, but he could never really understand what was going on inside of him. These inconsistent feelings were familiar and still…

He felt a soft touch on his left shoulder, gentle and chilly. He turned around mystified, for nobody was there with him except his unmoved friend. It was neither the wind nor the tree nor anybody who had come within reach of him, only a phantom touch that he could not make any sense of, that he had to have imagined. If he were religious, he might have explained it with an angel. But he wasn't. That would have been too nice because his belief embraced that he never really was alone. But he was sure that humans were alone. There were no god and no angels who kept watch over creation, or else he would not be sitting in this tree at that moment and be forsaken and on his own. Deep sadness filled him and wrapped him up. The loss was as fresh as the taste of the flesh of grapes on his tongue. He remembered.

Distant noises penetrated his consciousness gradually. He winced involuntarily and was startled out of his thoughts, already forgetting again. The noises were hardly louder than the murmur in the leaves at first and scarcely distinguishable from it. But they came closer, grew in intensity, and then at once he became aware of what it was: the menacing barking of a dog. But what seemed far worse to him was the fact that along with the animal a human came into his vicinity who would disconcert him in his last quiet minutes. He was riled and helpless. Hopefully, it passed quick and easy!

There was nothing else he could do except to wait and let it wash over him, if he wanted to remain unnoticed. Just don't come too close, he thought, but they did. The dog frolicked over the meadow in the twilight, barked eagerly and came close to the tree. The revolting sound of the animal roared in his head and drove away the last tones of flute. As if that wasn't enough already, it came worse: The owner of the dog left the path and followed the beast through the grass towards the tree.

He watched indignantly over the entire scene from his box seat. The dog turned around, leaped on one spot, ran over to his master, bounced in front of him, and the young man in his early twenties seemed to be amused about it!

It was the same young man whom he had seen here for the first time about a year ago and several times afterwards, one of the few who wandered to this place at all. The stranger often came in the late afternoon, but he did not come with the animal each and every time. Very rarely he strolled over the gravel path all by himself and kicked stones lost in thoughts. Never did he walk in human company.

This excessive cheerfulness of this young man was too much for him. It disturbed him, it derided him. He could not bear, if others behaved so happily. Often he would not even buy it. He was convinced that many people covered up their fears, sadnesses and sorrows with a friendliness simply put on. Everything seemed faked. Yet the stranger in his vicinity conveyed a feeling of naturalness which he could not grasp exactly. It probably originated from the contrast of what he had observed before. For the stranger appeared to have been initiated in the secret knowledge of sorrow as well, as he thought to have perceived from time to time in the last months.

Nevertheless, the current joyful outburst bothered him! He had wanted to bid farewell to his blushed friend, the security and the tranquillity of this place in peace. And then this anybody came along and destroyed everything! This was another proof that he wasn't granted any petty piece of happiness or personal rapture.

The bloke below giggled as the dog ran around him, once, twice, and then it ran in the direction of the tree. With a single clear laugh the stranger started to move to follow the animal.

He was sitting above in the tree top and saw the figure running towards him. Now it is over! Now he is going to see you! Close your eyes, hold your breath! It'll be over soon!

He took a deep breath and slowly his eyelids closed. The last sight before the darkness engraved itself in his memory:

the beaming visage of the stranger. He tried to dissipate this picture. The rustling steps of the two creatures through withered grass and fallen leaves stood out from the sighing of the wind. A laugh rang out and faded away. Then a squall chased through the oak tree's leafy canopy and whispered its song in the leaves. He felt the boughs defy the force of the storm and bend unwillingly. Then it became quieter. The wind eased off more and more. It was still. No noise anymore. Not even the flute in his head. No noise whatsoever anymore.

He slowly opened his eyes. The human and the animal were gone. He heaved a sigh of relief and marvelled, as the cool air streamed into his lungs. It felt as though he had not breathed in aeons. The time in which he had kept his eyes closed appeared now to have been infinitely long. He frowned and puckered his lips, turned his gaze to the side, hesitated pensively for a moment, then slightly shrugged his shoulders with resignation. He rubbed his cold hands against each other and relaxed his posture a bit because he had cowered frantically in expectation of his discovery.

A long sigh loosened from his inside. His farewell was scuppered, his perfect afternoon had been ruined in the end. He was not able to let in this feeling once again which had dominated him a short time ago. Instead his thoughts were with the peculiar stranger, whose face was still imprinted in his memory. As much as he tried to ban this picture, he did not succeed.

The sun was already deep on the horizon. He saw the reddish spark glint through the grey clouds. It was definitely time for him to leave. With limbs stiff with cold and from sitting for a long time, he climbed down from bough to bough, and from the lowest he swung down to the ground with elegant movements. As a friendly mien he pressed his lips together, said goodbye to the oak silently by embracing the trunk for some time, and thanked it for the refuge. He only dared to show this friendliness and closeness because there were no spectators and because he was convinced that he only attributed a personality, a soul to the tree, although in reality it did not possess anything like that.

Quickly he trudged over the meadow. The wind livened up and drove clouds from the west over his head. The breeze grasped him on the hilltop as it swept on eastwards. He looked to the horizon, the wind in his face, and stretched out his arms, his hands, his fingers and sensed the stream of air tear at him. The clouds in the sky broke open and the last fiery red rays of the setting sun touched his face. A tingling shudder ran down his spine. The glowing ball was already behind the far-away trees and only the upper edge peeked over them. While the sun was setting at last, the shadows of the forest crept up the hill of grass in his direction. When they had reached his feet, he looked down at himself and watched how the darkness clambered up his body. Soon the shadow was caressing his breast. He looked up again to the sun, which departed behind the trees. He lowered his eyes, closed them for a moment, then he turned on his heels and marched with long strides towards north-northeast.

The woods were murky, forsaken and scary in the twilight hour. A little fear took hold of him as usual. His adrenalin level rose. He was on the watch and prepared for a sudden attack of a wolf, although he was rather sure that nothing like that happened.

The stranger, whom he had forgotten about during the magnificent spectacle of nature, walked back into his con-sciousness. The exercising of his body made his thinking get a move on, too, and he reflected on the question why this young man had such a curious effect on him, why he seemed more congenial than the rest of humanity. After more than half an hour of brooding he passed the first house that stood secluded at the edge of the forest. He walked faster to get through the poorly lit streets to his dwelling as quickly as possible. He reached the anonymous housing block at the end of the last street of the suburb without noticing the pair of eyes watching him.

He walked the path along bushes to the entrance, rummaged in his pockets for the keys, unlocked the door and went to one of the flats on the fourth floor. Faint light shimmered through the spyhole. He opened the door and his mother, walking through the corridor, stopped, turned around and smiled at him.

"You arrived just in time. Supper is ready."

After he had discarded his stuff in his room and washed his hands, he sat down at the kitchen table with his mother. They ate silently for most of the time. The radio was quietly humming trivial pop music in the background as usual when they ate together. His mother looked up from her food now and again, looked in his direction, seriously and wearily. She tried to read his face or catch his glimpse to be able to start a conversation. He did not look up.

After the meal his mother complained, again as usual, about how little he had eaten. He helped her clean the dishes and deliberately ignored her complaints about work. She asked him a few questions about school and he answered in habitually brief words. As soon as he had stowed away the last crockery into the cupboard, he wished his mother a good night on the grounds that he still had to do some homework. In actuality, he lay down on his bed and dwelled on thoughts. He felt a little shattered. That was surely because of the temperature outside. He stood up to fetch his notebook and a pen. Lying on the bed he began to write a few words.

His mother went down the corridor to her bedroom. She must have been sitting in the living room and dozing there in front of the telly. Now she stopped in front of his door and listened for a while, then she went to her room and to bed.

He pitied her. She took care of him, worried about him. Her work was hard, tiring and paid poorly, but she did her best to allow them both to lead a life as comfortable as possible, although he was very modest. At the end of the week she was done in so much that she wanted nothing but peace all through the weekend to recover, only to be as exhausted on the second day of the new week as before the weekend. Slowly but surely she wore herself completely out. After work she did a little housework and apart from that she slept a good deal. That was one of the reasons why she did not have any friends or hobbies. She was leading a pitiable life, or rather a wretched, makeshift survival.

He might have helped her, supported her, could have made it easier for her. Surely this would have been the best for both of them. Maybe this way they would have had a better relationship to one another. But deep down he did not want it to be easy, as unfair as it was to his mother. Besides, he was fundamentally unable to walk back this path that he had taken after this crossroads of fate.

He continued to write. Once more he heard his mother going to the bathroom. He, too, was very tired by then. Soon he laid aside his writing utensils, undressed and went to bed as well. He cuddled his fleecy bedding and the two billowing pillows. He sighed. Until he fell asleep his mind spun around the face that appeared before him in the darkness. Something was different about these eyes…

Question of Point of View

I carry much too much encumbered load
and you are living your light-heartedness.
While I lie on the bottom smashed and bowed,
you're floating merrily without distress.

The many nothings I endured real tough
do press me heavily down in the dirt.
For you little everything's all enough,
it lifts you further away from my hurt.

When you are looking down on me in laze,
the world appears to be vast, fair and free.
When I to you above return the gaze,
the cry of the unhappy you don't see.

From your standpoint it's the big feast of life,
For me it's only nuisance, only strife.

2

The next morning was dull and very cold. Autumn roamed the country with wintry strands and caused uncomfortableness. The sky was dressed in clouds and hid the rising sun in its inside pocket from the eyes of mankind.

He woke up tired. His stereo system had come on fifteen minutes ago precisely at half past seven to wake him up with the inserted CD. It was one of the faster Rock songs playing now and it did not match his mood at all. He slumbered on for some more minutes, rolled around and around and snuggled up in his warm blanket, because he felt the cold in the room, menacing like a stranger at his bed.

This thought woke him fully. He opened his eyes. His room was pitch-dark, only the display of the equipment glowed. Even through the gaps of the shutters no light came in. This song bothered him enormously. He desperately wanted to turn it off, but he had to get up in order to do that. This idea, however, he liked even less. He would simply stay in bed the whole day pretending to be ill. Then he would not have to get up. But what if he needed to go to the loo? And could he really square with his own conscience not to go to school?

He rolled himself completely up under his cosy, fleecy blanket. Oh, how pleasant that was! Then, with brave determination he shoved the cover away from him and jumped out of bed. He went all goose-pimply and trembled softly. He did not feel particularly well.

His mother had left already. She always had to work early. He got ready, packed up his stuff, ate just a morsel, and left the flat, too, to go to school, which—conscientious as he was—he never wagged despite the temptation. Nevertheless, he was less than a little enthusiastic about the thought of going to this dreadful institution each and every morning afresh. He loathed school because of the mindless teachers, who held on to their curriculum without noticing that none of the pupils was the slightest bit interested, or who held on to their force-feeding, rattling-off teaching methods obstinately without noticing that not even a handful of interested pupils was able to follow. He loathed it because of the simple-minded pupils, who did not care one iota about learning something but rather indulged in their pubertal puerilities, who made bad jokes, played cheap tricks and schemed if they did not get what they wanted. If people were taken aback that they got harassed at work, then this was probably so because they had been brought up in a sheltered monastic school and did not have the faintest idea what real life was like and what it meant to be an outsider at an urban school.

Not that he took great pains to be accepted or integrated. No, he did not care about that at all. The few well-meant attempts of some of his classmates, well, the tossers of the class, he had pitilessly rebuffed. They bored him, all of them: the cool class favourites, the crawling swot, the good-natured mugs, the alternative stoners as well as the misfits. He only went to school out of necessity, sat down on his chair, listened, learned. And that was it! No friends, no tricks, nothing! That was exactly how he wanted it. This institution could have helped him to get out of life what he wanted. Most of his classmates strived for a good report, although most of them didn't do anything for it. The worst thing about it was that regardless of whether they worked hard for it or not, almost everybody came off well. The teachers' assessments were by no means just or adequate. He could have made an effort and been most excellent, but he did not want that. Although he was conscientious concerning his bodily presence because of compulsory schooling alone, but nobody could force him to anything that went beyond that. He feasted on this point.

As usual he pulled the lessons through, though he was only half-interested and rather bored, and then he went home. He had class until half past one, so he was home at about half past two. He ate a few sandwiches, leafed through the newspaper and afterwards whiled away the time loafing on his bed and listening to music, dabbling in homework and reading a book. The whole day long he had felt cold, even here in the flat. He had cold hands and feet. But instead of putting on something or turning on the heating, he accepted feeling cold, after all he was tough.

When his mother came back home shortly after six o'clock, they prepared supper together, consumed it silently, did the washing-up jointly and later watched a film together on the box which was not too bad. The living room was poorly lit, thus not adding more warmth to the room than the thermometer next to the balcony door indicated. They spoke very little in all that time which they spent together. Their evening together was a rarity, for he regularly withdrew to his room or was out and about, and she was mostly worn out from work. He was glad that she didn't ruin his uncommon concession by trying to start a conversation. They appreciated the peculiarity of this occasion even without talking much. Anyway, they had not had long conversations for years. Knowing that her son was reserved and had a mind of his own, that he might withdraw any second when she asked him about his life and tried to build up their relationship, his mother contained herself as well. Thus their life took the same mindless course over and over again.

His mother only mentioned, shortly before going to bed, that it would be nice if the two of them went on an outing together some time. She had said the very same thing too often without anything coming of it. Therefore he did not really take it seriously. The two of them were no idyllic family, rather they shared a flat. Both went about their own ways, which met every now and then. This had become too much of a habit to break it. Besides, he was not sure whether he sincerely would have wanted to do something with her if she had made a serious move. Maybe he would have taken pity on her if she had wished so with determination. She had not been out for years, except for a few family parties on big birthdays of distant relatives. His mother looked very miserable. They both felt how far they had become estranged from each other and left it at that.

After his mother had gone to bed and all was quiet, he lay down on his bed and began to write into the night.

Emotional Distance

Your wings lie shattered on the floor,
Buried is your heart thereunder infinitely deep.
You are dazed about the birds
Flying high in the skies above.

The height that they reach
You will never gain,
If you don't unleash your heart.

The freedom of the heavens high
Is both enticing and frightening,
For you lie on the ground so low.
Unbelievable, one can be so strong
To soar up to these heights!

Your lack of faith in yourself
Is what keeps your heart chained up.

3

He awoke early the following morning, tired and grumpy. His desire not to have to go to school was even greater than the day before. He asked himself why he did not simply stay at home. His mother would not notice it. The teachers would, but what difference did it make if it was just this one time?

To be sure he did get up. After he had got ready in the bathroom, had taken a small, insufficient breakfast, and had thrown his school supplies into his rucksack, he strolled to the bus in order to go to school. The other people in the streets looked equally tired, sluggish and unenthusiastic. Only the lower forms were in high spirits, lively romping around the schoolyard, running around and screaming loudly.

The first periods were awfully boring and tiresome. He sucked listlessly at a bottle of water he had taken with him not to fall asleep. To drink much additionally allowed him to retreat from this unpleasant bunch more frequently, if only for a short time. His seat was next to the window and he derived more pleasure from watching out of it and switching off his thoughts than from following class. He stared at the sky, but could not perceive a change of its grey. The history teacher was busy with letting the class read old texts which she called historically most fascinating.

During break he stood towards the side of the hallway far off from the others and continued to suck at his water. It was empty halfway through the break. He did not let the hustle and bustle in the hallway disturb him, instead he daydreamed. The third period passed him by unnoticed and the fourth tormented him again with boredom.

Shortly before the end of the fourth one, in which they were having mathematics, the water he had knocked back made itself felt. His urge to pass it grew stronger and stronger, but he tried to ignore it and sit through it until the next break. He stared out of the window, fidgeted about on his chair more and more, crossed his legs. It was no use! Five minutes before the break bell rang he had to get up and leave the classroom to go to the toilette. Normally he would not have left in the very last minutes of class. This was indication for the urgency. Yet the teacher did not know about it and looked at him reproachfully while he went to the door.

When he returned, the teacher was already gone, unusually early. He had missed the assignment of homework. If the teacher had still been there, he had asked him about it, of course, but in this situation he only had two possibilities: either not to do homework at all or to ask one of his classmates, which generally was out of the question. Double bind!

Obeying his sense of duty he opted for the latter solution. Many of his classmates had left the room for the break even before the teacher. Only a few of the girls had stayed behind and were chattering. Hesitantly he walked towards the group and asked Caroline what the teacher had assigned for them. She specified a couple of exercises from their book. The other girls were giggling the whole time through, looking at each other. It seemed a bit dubious to him, but Caroline was a scrupulous girl in his estimation. He had to believe her whether he liked it or not if he did not want to ask others. And that he definitely did not want! This was unpleasant enough for him.

The last period did not seem to end at all. Time passed by so slowly that it had almost crawled backwards. Finally the school bell rang and he could leave the school behind. He set out for home straightaway. The roistering children were jarring on him. He did not want to stand them any second longer than needed.

Having arrived back home, he cooked a serving of pasta, which he dressed with ketchup, and sat down with it at his writing desk. With dangling legs he chewed on the soft spirals apathetically, flicked through the latest newspaper and skimmed the headlines. He had stopped caring about wars, disaster, epidemics or political affairs a long time ago. It did not have any effect on his life anyway whether a coach had an accident in Spain or a woman had killed her husband in the most brutal way in South Africa or what some Presidential candidate promised during his campaign. In the end he wouldn't keep it anyway. He rolled his eyes because of the sensational headlines. Such a humbug, all of it! What did it mean for his life if a village in Russia had been flooded? Globalization produced strange effects in his view. Then again it was almost amusing, this study of mankind. Then it dawned on him. What kind of news from all around the world did the newspapers print? Only reports about catastrophes, sowing fear and horror into the minds of readers. As if no one was interested in all the good things that had happened in the world. Oh, okay, the oldest learner driver of France finally got her driving licence after one hundred and seventy lessons, if that was important to anyone. Was there nothing positive besides that to report on? Did the world really want to know all the negative, the worst, and drug itself with it? So and so many people have lost their homes or even their lives? Look here: Another Afro-American was shot by a white police officer in the U.S.! Still war in the Middle East, or again! Did yet another plane crash? No, not today, or rather yesterday to be precise. But a prison in Caracas had burned, as news got abroad, and a death penalty had been enforced in China! Thank goodness, how lucky we are to live in such a secure country! Oh, what a great life we have! If only there weren't four million people unemployed, as many as never before, the ever-growing gap between rich and poor in general, sky-rocketing cancer rates, food scandals, all kinds of environmental pollution, acid rain, forest dieback and so forth! No, man wasn't good, neither to their habitat, their fellow beings nor to themselves or their bodies. But hell no, none of these pollutions had anything to do with all of this! Misery lived just around the corner and the people had to lie to themselves in order to not notice that they probably weren't that well-off after all. Had he discovered another grand delusion of mankind?

Or was it perhaps that the world should be held in anxiety and terror, so that it was easier to be controlled, so that it consumed, so that it was kept busy lest it dealt with the truly important things in life? Frightened people took out expensive insurance, of which they actually hoped that they never had to claim it. Frightened people relinquished their most fundamental rights for their security and were contented that the state, that good old gaffer, sheltered them from exploitations, terrorists, plagues, from each and every menace—however hazy they might be! The media repeated everything as long as even the last critic believed it and conformed. Bread and circuses—and opium—for the world, so that the actual decision-makers had free reign!

Solely an article in the feuilleton allured him: a review of his favourite actor's latest film. They scorched the movie, wrote that he was a ghastly actor, who had better become a butcher. What did they know? They did not have the feel for the highly sensitive and profound performance of this exceptional character actor. The world misjudges true genius, he said to himself.

The movie opened in cinemas today. That was brilliant, he rejoiced, because today he had plenty of time. Like every day. So he would treat himself and go to the movies. He was alone anyway, as his mother came back home later. He did his homework unhurriedly, calmly, wrote a note to his mother, placed it on the kitchen table and headed towards the city centre in the later afternoon.

He had to walk roughly ten minutes to the next bus stop and missed the bus by inches. But he had enough time and the next bus was to come ten minutes later. Fortunately, two lines going to the centre via different routes stopped here. The faster and quieter one he had just missed. At least At least he had the opportunity to behold the grey facades of the houses, the ill-kempt, littered green space behind the station and the few passers-by during this time. Certainly he was all too familiar with that, yet it remained a mystery to him how people could be so heedless to throw their litter half a metre besides a municipal bin. This neighbourhood was completely run-down. This was due to the people and the rampant indifference, presumably due to underpaid jobs and the negative propaganda of the media.

The bus was late, as it was to be expected from the trans-portation company, though it had just started its route and was almost devoid of any passengers. It was an articulated bus and he sat down backwards in the front part directly at the joint. Thus he could observe everything that happened in the rear part. He already knew what was awaiting him: Several stops after he got on the bus, a pack from the comprehensive school boarded and pressed into the rearmost part of the bus. They were louts, proles, who had to prove themselves. They shouted at each other, pushed each other, made a fool of each other and themselves and rampaged around as if they had been released from gag arrest. He did not have a clear idea about comprehensive school but when he looked at the scene unfurling before his eyes then the only reasonable explanations for such behaviour were that it really was like a prison, or that the label 'comprehensive school' was euphemistic for lunatic asylum or anti-social safe-keeping institution.

Most of them went to the city centre too. Because he could not stand them any longer, he got off one stop before the town hall and ambled along the shopping street. People hurried past him with rigid, mask-like grimaces on their faces and tense postures, heavy bags in their hands or heavy burdens on their shoulders. They hastened, shoved and grumbled. These were indisputable symptoms of hurried-ness, unhappiness and mental dullness. The wind blew even colder through the streets of the city than in front of his house, and the sky was gloomy and dusky. For this reason the peoples' faces were even greyer.

It was one of the smaller arthouse cinemas where his path led him. He was right with his conjecture that none of the large multiplexes would screen a film like the one he wanted to see. From afar he could read the old-fashioned lettering: "WILTED FLOWERS" was billed there with big old plastic letters in black between black bars in front of white backlit plastic panes underneath the cinema logo. Two tardy people were buying tickets for one of the two more lowbrow movies at the box office. After he had bought his ticket, he entered the pretty empty, but splendid pre-war foyer, at the entrance of which a few posters hung and an out-dated, bleached-out cardboard advertisement stood. An employee behind a counter handed out ice cream and change to the couple and yawned without holding his hand in front of his mouth, when they had turned and strolled to the largest auditorium, afterwards he looked at his dirty fingernails. He knew that the earlier screenings were rather boring and hardly anyone bought popcorn, sweets or beverages.

He walked past the bar, darted the employee an indifferent, maybe even slightly disgusted glance, and disappeared through the right door into the medium-sized cinema hall. It was dark. He needed a short moment for his eyes to get used to the darkness, yet still he felt his way a few steps forwards. Due to the missed and the late busses, the commercials were already on. Against the illuminated screen he could see the silhouettes of unoccupied seating running row after row, slightly sloping downwards towards the screen. Nevertheless one would not be able to see the screen, if someone big sat right in front.

He chose a seat in the very centre of the hall in order to sit not too far away from the picture, for the screen was much too small for the hall anyway, and then again not to get a stiff neck. After three more spots the commercials were over and the light went on for two minutes. This was the last chance to spend one's money after that constant stream of partisan consumer counselling. Maybe in the olden days someone had now been walking through the hall pushing a cart and selling ice cream and beverages. No one took the troubles nowadays because of the hardly present customers. Who'd want to watch this film anyhow? The main light went out and the projectionist started the reel, before which two tedious and supremely boring trailers had been cut. When eventually these were over too, the last dim lights on the side walls went out and left him alone with the film.

He enjoyed his favourite actor's performance for way more than two hours, who once again was grand. He loved to stay in these big dark halls all alone without being bothered by the chuckling, chewing or canoodling of others. The way it was right now, largest-possible visual and acoustic spectacle, which he couldn't experience at home, all for himself, that was how cinema was fun! There was nobody blocking his view and nobody who could distract his attention away from the film with whatsoever. He lost himself in the story, which was told for him and him alone.

The end.

The final melody began to play, the cast scrolled up the screen in the order of appearance and the hall's faint side lighting went on.

He sat up again, after he had sunk deeper and deeper and more comfortably into his chair during the film. His right leg had gone to sleep and now prickled wildly. He gave his calf a massage for a minute, but it did not help. Therefore he stretched his arms and the upper part of his body, reached for his jacket and rose to leave the cinema. Every time he trod on his right foot, his leg started to pinch and tingle anew. He walked down the row to the aisle on the left side, where he stopped and stayed. The whole time he looked at the screen as if he was mesmerised. Ultimately all of these listed names were of absolutely no use to him, but still he considered it a kind of appreciation, because in conclusion they all had contributed their mite to the film, even if only as a driver, caterer or boom operator. The used songs were detailed not before the very end. It irritated him for whatever reason that the music was always last. When a song had been appealing, one had to wait and watch the complete end titles to learn who had performed it. And then two or three titles were placed next to each other and rolled over the screen at such a pace that one could not find the right title that quickly nor write it down hastily enough. This annoyed him, although for the most time he stayed until the very end anyway. Was the music held in such a low regard by the filmmakers? That bothered him, although he usually stayed until the end. Most of the audience was gone by then. This film however had only an orchestral score, which he wouldn't buy.

The curtain was drawn and the main light went on. He turned away from the screen and he was to make towards the exit, but then he hesitated for a seemingly excessively long moment of shock. He was not alone! The stranger rose from one of the seats in the back rows to leave the cinema as well. Coolly and yet shocked he pulled his jacket tighter around the shoulders and whooshed along the aisle in order to escape the sharp eyes of the stranger. His gaze directed towards his shoes, his strides flew over the ascending carpet flooring, racing like his heart incited by adrenalin. He could already make out the dark door, which was promising rescue. A black trainer penetrated his field of vision from the side, then a second. That was the stranger! He looked up to him, although he did not want to. The young man looked at him a little bit absentmindedly, but benignantly.

"Such a surprise…"

Oh no! Did he recognise him? Certainly, certainly!

"I thought I was alone in this film", stuttered the stranger.

Relief! He did not know!

But how did he not see his head protruding over the rows of seats?

"Me neither…" His reply passed his lips more dismissively than he had intended. But then he was out through the door, certain that it closed on the other one's face. Through the dapper entrance hall, which was packed a little more for the evening screening, past the box office and out into the nightly cold air he dashed. He rushed through the hardly antsy streets. The shops were closed, takeaways and restaurants catered to hungry people inside, many a pub was swarming and noisy, some kiosks sold tobacco and alcohol—

everything one needed at night. His feet and lungs burned because of the needlessly rushed flight from the stranger, who had come dangerously close to him. He only slowed down his stride after he had almost collided with a woman at the last corner on his way to the bus stop where he meant to get on.

This time he boarded the bus in the front and also sat down more towards the front. In the nightly hours the buses waited for each other at this central stop to guarantee customers to change. For this reason nothing moved for nearly ten minutes, then several busses started their engines at practically the same time and went about their routes in all directions.

His glance was directed to the world outside the window, but his thoughts were focussed on his inside. He brooded over the film, which had agitated him to some extent. The story about the lonesome, disabled person who had achieved something in life and had finally found friends after years of loneliness had been told empathetically and encouragingly, so that he would have had identified himself with it too willingly. But to what should he let himself be encouraged? He was neither physically nor mentally disabled, merely and simply socially, and therefore he should not let the film give him any silly notions, he cautioned himself. Furthermore he did not particularly like the depiction of bodily deformity. That stoked his fear of contact somehow and caused internal discomfort.

Trying to ban these thoughts, he had to think about this unexpected encounter with the stranger. This had thrown him out of balance. It vexed him that he had been talked to; but even more that he had almost lost his self-control, if he had not opted for flight, and that he had been so rude against the stranger. It was all so contradictory. Because who forbid him to be friendly provided that someone was friendly to him? Yet this wasn't allowed! In point of fact he did not want to ponder this either and pushed this brooding aside. However, the more he fought against them, the stronger these thoughts came back into his mind. Thankfully he was only two stops away from where he had to get off.

Practical as he was, he got up when the bus had already stopped, and slipped skilfully through the front door which just opened. As he had to walk a few metres back, he saw everybody getting off through the rear door. As a matter of course the stranger was among those. Many of them crossed the street and a few walked in front of him, but disappeared into the houses by and by. The stranger, however, walked on and on in front of him, even when nobody else was there anymore, but did not turn around. He probably knew that he was walking behind him. The stranger strode quite slowly, more slowly than he himself would normally have walk, but he wanted to stay behind the stranger, so that he didn't have to overtake him eventually. That was too embarrassing. Therefore he accommodated his speed to that of the young man and kept his distance.

In short distance to his housing complex he turned into a side street. Only then did their ways part, for the stranger kept straight on. Looking back he saw in which of the houses the stranger disappeared, hardly three stone's throws away from his own building. Although they lived close by, he had never encountered him outside of the woods for a year.

His mother had already gone to bed, although it was still reasonably early. He read for an hour, before he lay down to sleep. This night he could not find sleep for a long time. His thoughts kept him awake.

Thoughts About You

Rain lashes me in the face.
The sun's light,
by clouds subdued,
makes the city look
grey and dreary.
I flee from the noise,
the turmoil.
The silvan foliage,
discoloured complying with the season,
defies the rain drum
nevermore,
dropping, falling, owing
to the added weight.

I return
to my childhood's place,
our secret space.
In the almost mouldered tree
house I sit down
and to the flood
of memories surrender.

The thoughts about you
are the only happy ones,
left over from a past
that I displaced.
More real than ever
you appear to me.
The hope to meet you again
makes me ride out the bleak routine.

Every minute I thought about you,
but your face faded away in time.

I am here now
to retrieve you
in the hope
to enable the puzzle
of my past to recompose,
to find out the mystery
of my condition.

4

Thursday morning, the last day of October. His humour had hit rock-bottom, but still he did not give up and decided to be strong and to stick out the day till the last. After all, he had done the homework and this should not have been in vain.

While leaving the house he realised that this day was to be simply dreadful. It was cold again and it started to rain on his way to the bus station. The jacket he wore did not have a hood, but getting another coat or an umbrella was too laborious, he thought. As a consequence he ran through the rain to the stop as fast as he could. The windowpanes of the heated bus were steamed up because of the high humidity from the vaporised dampness of the passengers' clothes.

In the crush of rain refugees and umbrellas in the schoolyard, three of the younger pupils ran square to him. The first held something in his hand and waved it to and fro. The second tried to wrench it from his hand. The third one laughed and yelled again and again: "To me, to me!" The first bore down straight on him. He was fast and, despite of this, did not pay attention where he was running, because he was preoccupied to withhold the loot from their victim. He came closer and closer. On the last few metres he finally turned around, became aware of what was about to happen and sidestepped on the boggy lawn screamingly, yet still in due time. Otherwise the brat had bowl him over anyhow. His own fault if he got his shoes and trousers dirty!

Startled, the lass behind him leapt aside and fell into the strong arms of her boyfriend, fortunately, who was in the final year and walked next to her. The near jostler tumbled and slipped on the slick sludge, landed prone in the dirt and slid a bit further, now soiled over and over with mud.

At least there was a little bit of justice in this world, he contemplated. The villain ends on the ground and the girl in the arms of the hero. Still he was peeved by this superfluous action.

The first lesson, religion, went by without any further incidents. In the second, however, which was mathematics, the next rout of the day came: The homework he had done was the wrong one—as was to be expected— and besides that much too much. The teacher was merciless and did him down in front of the whole class. Caroline and her girl-friends, just like everybody else, found it highly amusing.

He was the only one to remain at his seat during break after this period. He could hear the others laughing at him. Some of them positioned themselves pretty insolently near him and laughed at him openly, barefacedly. He pretended not to notice any of that, but it did hurt, and that was very hard to harbour in spite of all his years of practise. He had believed that, after such a long time of being uninvolved in this class, nobody bore an interest in twitting him, ridiculing him. He had believed that he was so unimportant that nobody wasted a thought about him. Obviously he was not insignificant enough to not become the victim of vicious pranks. He still was the alien body in the class. This had been more than evident before, but now he would have to draw the obvious conclusion. After he had always got off cheaply in the last years, he now had to reckon with becoming the object of new cruelties in the near term, for example being the target for projectiles like chalk or wet sponges or finding drawing pins on his chair.

The class calmed down a little in the next double period and they left him alone. He felt inadequate nevertheless. Why had he been so stupid to trust anybody? He should have known better not to do so.

During the next break he sat a little bit away from the schoolyard under eaves, because it was still drizzling. There he took a very small book, which was halfway tattered as if it had been read a thousand times, out of his rucksack. He opened it on the first pages and started to read:

Bernardo: Who's there?

Francisco: Nay, answer me: stand, and unfold yourself.

Bernardo: Long live the king!

Francisco: Bernardo?

Bernardo: He.

Francisco: You come most carefully upon your hour.

Bernardo: 'Tis now struck twelve; get thee to bed, Francisco.

Francisco: For this relief much thanks: 'tis bitter cold, and I am sick at heart.

He liked the last sentence. The beginning of the book was quite fine, and the next pages went on excitingly. One had to congratulate Shakespeare for it. It was about a terrifying apparition, which had been seen twice, but which still was beyond belief. And then the ghost appeared again, this time in the presence of his son. His impression was that he would love Hamlet this time again. The language alone was excellent.

Because he was so riveted by his reading and because he sat too far aside, he did not hear the bell at the end of the break. Only ten minutes later did he become aware of the fact that the clamour and the frolicking had ceased. He must have appreciated the silence too much. Startled he sprang up slamming the book shut and darted to and through the building to the physics room. Having reached it, he heard the appalling voice of the much hated and feared teacher through the door painted green. He paused for a moment, took a deep breath, for he was out of breath, and then he entered the room somewhat calmer. All the attention was directed at him. Everything was quiet; even the teacher had interrupted his speaking. Great, now he had the unpleasant, unwelcome attention of everyone! This was something that he otherwise knew how to avoid.

The teacher looked at him but did not say a word. Therefore he considered sitting down at one of the free seats in the vexing front row. But before he reached the chair, the teacher shook off his uncredulity about this impudent impertinence.

"Where do you come from? How do you dare come too late? Where were you?"

He preferred to not say a thing and simply to endure the hue and cry. He already felt bad enough, so he did not need a scene so encouraging.

"This is not okay and earns you a bad mark. Coming late and interrupting the whole lesson. And that without any reason." The teacher looked at him sternly and amplified the tension by a deliberate long pause, ere he continued with a frosty tone: "Or do you have a cogent reason for this?"

He lowered his eyes, with which he had bravely returned the teacher's stare so far, but did not answer. He had already known that Mr Angerman was remorseless, pitiless, but that he made such a big fuss about being late once he had not anticipated. The teacher could have proceeded without being bothered about it. Others were able to do that all the same. But apparently he had just sought for a reason. He had not disturbed the lesson, but the teacher had interrupted it. Then he remembered again: Many a time Mr Angerman had bellowed at pupils unfoundedly, and on several occasions it had seemed as if he was about to strangle that person.

He felt miserable. His head was thumping and his stomach cramped. And what was about to follow gave him the final stab in the back. Someone from the back rows said unsolicitedly:

"I have seen him down there. He had been reading and ignoring the bell deliberately."

That was a lie! It had been a mistake. And why on earth did they interfere in other people's affairs! The teacher looked around the room searchingly, trying to spot the one who had spoken, then devoting himself again to him and the book which he was still holding in his hand.

"Hamlet, I see. Well, at least a classic. Yet this is not the literature class, but physics. And it looks as if you won't pass this course. This means: no qualifications! Or do you believe you know your stuff? Then please come to the front and demonstrate your knowledge!"

That was it! He was well aware of the fact that he was about to fail, aware that this spelled the end for him. He did not want to go to the front, but the teacher repeated his request and he complied with it, albeit grudgingly. He went to the front to the blackboard, picked up a piece of chalk and wrote down what the teacher dictated. Then he stood in front of the assignment and did not know what to do with it, which was not only due to his frame of mind, but which was also related to the fact that this class had never before dealt with this topic. He was being humiliated maliciously.

"What's the matter? Are you too dense for this task?", jibed the teacher, and his classmates chuckled amused. "Get a move on, Hamlet!"

And then it happened: Something inside of him broke. He felt it most clearly. It was a burst that only he was able to hear, a rip that only he could feel. It hurt and he was on the brink of bursting into tears. He was destroyed! But he pulled himself together in his ultimate desperation and stood still, fixating on the teacher. For a while they duelled with their gazes, and then the teacher relented: "Now sit yourself down! That was absolutely pathetic!"

He sat down in the front row and felt the burning stares in his back. And then, all of a sudden, a grey shroud drew over him and cocooned him. Everything became surreal and moved away from him. His ally took him in his protective embrace and he knew that the pain held him safely. He forgot everything around him, suddenly felt free and light-hearted, as if he was in a soap bubble which kept everything at bay. Nothing reached him anymore. He did not perceive anymore how the gleefully gloating giggling was called a halt by the steely words of the teacher, nor how the lesson elapsed nor how afterwards he grabbed his stuff and left school behind. Neither did he notice that he would skive off the last two periods. The soap-bubble state felt warm and safe, although the weather was cold and stormy, and like in a trance it wafted him home, where he emptied out his school supplies from his bag and packed up a few things without thinking about it.

He did not even feel how his feet carried him out of the house, through the streets and into the forest, up the hill to the oak. It rather appeared to him as if he was floating there. What's more, he did not feel how it started to rain in the forest, after it had stopped raining in the course of noon-time. The drops drummed on the leaves which were still hanging on the tree as well as on his head. His head felt empty.

When he reached the tree, he took something out of his bag, which he put down at the moist but somewhat shel-tered trunk of the oak. He climbed up into the top, sat down on one of the high boughs and began to work with his hands with proficient yet unknown movements. Only after he had finished his activity, did a tiny splinter of consciousness slip back into this world, and he apprehended what he had just done. It made him smirk. In his hands he held a solid noose, which he had made from his mother's skipping rope. This irony was relieving despite of the situation.

He knew now what he had to do. For years he finally had a real aim, an aspiration, something that would at long last give him the quietude which he had longed for eagerly for so long. Even if there had been a god, he could not have hindered him from his execution with all his hosts of angels. So this was his destination and he would gladly bow to it. He knotted the noose tightly to the branch on which he was sitting, a smile on his face. Even his eyes smiled in anticipation of what was about to happen.

There, there it was again, the flute in his head! It played again its song rife with dolour and melancholy. And wasn't there a voice singing with the flute? It really was a voice, soothing and deep. Mournfully and gently it expressed the wounds of his soul with its lugubrious chant, saying farewell. The cold wind whistled his winter song thereto. He asked it to take him along, wherever it was blowing to. Bear me away from here!

He made sure that the rope was strong and would not tear or the knot unfasten. This was it, the moment that he had been awaiting, the moment that he had envisioned in his mind just like this and not a bit differently, the moment that his whole existence had been heading for. It was perfect. Now he was able to let himself go at last.

For a last time he regarded the meadow, the landscape, the forests, the motorway, the pylons and the city in his back. Would he miss this life and regret it? Certainly not! Would he remember it? Who in this world knew beforehands, but probably not. He closed his eyes, imagined the world as it kept on turning without taking any note of his termination.

He listened carefully to the music within him. A violin had taken over the farewell melody, rending, breaking his heart. It reprised the theme of his life and his end and weaved these two together. He pictured in his mind's eye a dreamworld, the happy life that he had never had and never could have had: a family, friends, joys, hopes, trust. He saw the bridge which had been demolished in his past and which had led into this world now out of his reach. Well well, both worlds would soon collapse and vanish, cease to be.

For once and for all, it was time for him to go, time for his walk in the clouds. He silently thanked God, destiny or coincidence, to who or whatever he owed his distressed, hard-to-take life. Chosen it himself he had definitely not. Wherever it hailed from, however it had taken its course, this all became past now. He reached for the noose in order to put it around his neck...

...when suddenly the barking of a dog sounded and startled him so much that he almost fell off the tree. He opened his eyes in disbelief. Indeed, the cur ran over the meadow. He was stricken by horror. He would get busted. He would be discovered in time and be saved if he did it now. Damn, his backpack still leaned at the tree's trunk to betray him. He had to do something about it, to hide the bag and himself and to continue later. He repented having placed his stuff down there so thoughtlessly, so carelessly. A short while ago it had seemed useful. Who could have reckoned that someone came here at this time and in this weather?

The animal had descried his bag, at least it ran straight towards the tree. Quick-wittedly he clawed his way down from branch to branch in order to possibly get there first, get hold of his belongings and to hide them. Meanwhile, on one of the lower boughs he saw that the human, the stranger under an umbrella, was already quite close.

He clambered on a branch on the far side of the mighty trunk lest he be seen. What else was he supposed to do? To save his rucksack meant to reveal himself to the stranger. If someone discovered him here with his scheme and hindered him to bring it to completion, then questions about what his intention was and who he was weren't far ahead. He would surely be interrogated about his reasons and his past. Maybe this bloke would call the police as a precaution and thereby sic a psychologist on him subsequently. They would interrogate him regarding his reasons and his past, perhaps institutionalise him, treat him with electroshocks and strong psychotropic drugs. If, on the other hand, he backed off and remained unnoticed, the stranger would in all probability take his bag and with it his most important treasure: the file with his manuscripts, his complete works of poetry and fiction, pages upon pages filled with his life and his thoughts, the life's work. He must not lose this for any price! Even if what he had written did not make any sense isolated from his life, still it belonged to him and should not be taken away from him.

The young man came closer and closer.

"What have you found there, Ellie? A backpack? What does it do here?" the stranger wondered, then stutteringly shouted into the wind, "Hello, is there anyone?"

He was on the horns of a dilemma: No matter for which he decided, his manuscripts or his remaining undetected, he had to sacrifice the other inevitably. On which of these two should his decision fall? If he accomplished his plan, he would not be able to take his collected words with him, wherever he went. But they meant too much to him while he still lived. They were the only thing in the whole world

44

that meant anything to him. This collection of manuscripts was a part of himself.

Blimey, what should he do? How should he decide? His thoughts ran at full steam. What should he do?

"It seems there is nobody here. Shall we leave the backpack here or take it with us, Ellie? If someone has left it, he will surely look for it here. But then, if it lies here longer, it will soak through."

The stranger did not stutter anymore. Did he only do that if he was nervous or insecure, in the presence of other people? He did not have any more time to think about it, for he heard that the stranger opened his bag and rustled in it. What the hell should he do now? For what should he decide: rucksack or his unrecognised identity? What, confound it!

"There's only a file with a lot of paper in it, and some odds and ends", the stranger reported to his pooch need-lessly.

His spontaneous impetus was that he wanted to scream, wanted to jump off the tree and grab his things. All at once he felt giddy, then everything went black. A soft moan passed his lips, but the wind carried it away unheard. His consciousness played a trick on him. Before he was able to make a conscious decision, an unknown instance of his self usurped the leading role and cheated him out of his destiny. That was not how he had conceived it.

"Okay, you're right, I will take it and we bring it to the police. But then we go back and deliver it immediately." The dog leapt up and down. Animal and human left the finding place, the bag thrown casually over the shoulder.

He recovered from his blackout. He hung on one of the lower boughs crampedly and a wave of frustration blew upon him. He had been betrayed by himself and the stranger had his manuscripts now. He also felt forsaken by his friend, the oak, for it had not provided the shelter it had promised him.

He could not tarry at this place of his greatest defeat. Therefore he jumped down from the lowest branch to the ground, landed wobbly on his feet and left the tree behind. The overall result was extremely disenchanting. His soap bubble had burst. Just now for the first time he became aware that he was totally drenched by the rain. It had almost stopped raining in the meantime, but in return the wind was blowing even colder than before. He shivered all over and felt miserable, pulled his jacket closer around him, so that drops were wrung from it. It could not warm him.

Over the meadow and through the forest he dragged himself, gasping and groaning. His aggravation was beyond measure. Just why had he allowed this to happen? Why had he betrayed himself? Everything was lost. His life could not have been any more useless. Actually he could have let himself go much more easily now, but living on was the only sensible punishment for his shortcoming. Every escape would only have been an abscondence from justice. Oh, blast it, he felt so dreadfully cold! His teeth were chattering. Atrocious was the cold, which lamed him like the vacuity. He struggled to walk at all.

He had already dragged himself quite a distance through the woods, when he heard the scrunching of steps behind the trees to his left. With violent effort he increased his pace. His legs stung and were heavy. His throat was on fire. A slimy taste of iron was in his mouth. He coughed momentarily.

A fork turned up in front of him and the stranger's dog trotted towards him between the trees. When he reached the fork and the tame animal reached him, he saw the silhouette of a person coming up to him on the left path;

this had to be the young man, who had turned back following the dog.

"Hey there, please excuse me!", yelled the stranger stammeringly.

He stopped and stared into space trying to hide his pale face and his trembling lips in the shadows.

"Of course, you are excused", he replied.

The stranger came closer with every step.

"What's the matter with you? You are totally drenched. You don't look good at all."

Without looking at the stranger directly, he pointed to the rucksack shakily: "That's mine."

"I didn't know that. I just…"

"May I have it back?"

"Oh, of course, wait!" The young man stopped in front of him and unshouldered the bag. He held it out to him, and he reached for it. As soon as he clutched it with his hand, he sank to the ground…

Is This Death?

The rain is drumming against the pane.
I get up and
draw the curtain away.
The trees bend in the storm.
I don't know the season.
I go outside and
feel the force of nature.
The wind plays with my hair,
plays with my wet hair.
The storm moves quickly.
The clouds, they are so dark.
A thunderbolt flashes,

falls to the ground
– for a moment it is possible
to see the surrounding,
then it is dark again.
Even my life seems to be in the dark.
I lift my arms to the sky
and scream as loud as I can.
Another lightning.
I feel it coming.
I feel weak,
sink to the ground.
I wish that this is death!
Oh, how I wish that this is death!

5

A soft lap came to his ears. He felt warm and light momentarily, almost weightless. Forgotten were his problems which had plagued him before. He was secure at this dark place where the lapping was close and all around him. This was surely Styx, the river of the underworld, which the shadows of the deceased souls had to cross. It, the hated, was not only a myth, but it was reality, the real river of hate.

He was well able to recollect the last occurrences which had happened before he had sunk down: He had got back his bag from the stranger. This must have redeemed him, for thus he had the obol which he had to pay Charon, the demonic ferryman of souls, in order to be brought across the Styx without having to wait one hundred long years. His manuscripts were no doubt an adequate boatage. Nowadays these things were surely more valuable than the coin which was formerly placed underneath the tongue of the dead. Was this the secret?

Strangely enough he could not remember what had happened after his breakdown. Had he met Charon yet? Was he sitting in his boat? Or was he already on the other side, in the unseen house of Hades?

Certainly he was in the underworld. But it smelled much more pleasant here, contrary to his expectations, of herbs or pine. He could not identify it exactly. Had someone blindfolded him so that he could not find his way back into the world of the living? He could not see anything at all. Or was this place actually so pitch-dark? Of course, this region was called Erebos, the Darkness. This name had not been chosen haphazardly.

Something splashed next to him and he was grasped at the forearm. Was this the hand of Charon, who would soon guide him a bit further? Did the old ferryman want to help him to get out of his boat? He was getting a little bit nervous concerning the indistinctness of what was about to happen furthermore. He waited some time, but nothing happened. He was still held at the wrist, but not the slightest inclination to lead him was shown. What was wrong?

Thereupon his wrist was released, it splashed once again, and steps clattered, moved away, and resounded from a distance. He was being left alone once again. He did not understand. He fretted himself about it. Was he to follow in the direction where the steps had faded away? Up to now he had not moved a bit. Maybe this was exactly what was expected of him.

He tried hard to move, but his limbs were tired, languid and heavy, and it took him a lot of strength to even turn his head ever so slightly in the direction where the sounds had faded away. It felt peculiar. The right side of his face perceived an alteration which he could not explain accurately. It was very odd, as if a perpendicular border was traversing over his face. He lifted his hand towards his face. It was heavy, and it too sensed an unmistakable, cool and strange change and became instantaneously heavier. There was a babble, and when his hand came close to his face, drops splashed on his nose and cheeks. There was something odd here.

Immediately it all became clear to him. He opened his eyelids, which were so light and yet so heavy. He had to squeeze his eyes shut right away, then he blinked and found himself, after his eyes had adjusted to the dull light, in a tub in a brightly tiled room. The greenish water, in which he was lying, was warm and steamed slightly. A tenuous, soft but warm illumination was provided by several candles, which were distributed all over the room.

Feeble as he was he wondered where he was, how he had got to this place and what all of this meant. At least one thing was obvious now: The whole thing about Styx, Charon and all of that nonsense was nothing more than a fixed idea. He was neither dead nor in the underworld. But somebody had been here, someone who must have brought him hither. Somebody must have found him lying in the woods… and brought him somewhere… He assumed that it must have been the stranger, who had stood right in front of him. But where was this where? Could this be a hospital? No, he did not think so. This place lacked the typical tang and the distinctive look of hospitals. Not that he had been in a hospital often enough, but he had made a pertinent experiences that one time that he had been in one himself after a serious accident. It seemed rather as if he were in the stranger's home.

Anyway! He should rather find out how the land lied, he advised himself. Since nobody sojourned in this room, he had to draw attention to himself. Should he call? He was weak and his throat felt sore and dry. To call seemed too strenuous. He could wait. Most probably the stranger or this someone would soon come to see after him.

And so it happened. Not long since he heard a low shuffling approaching him without him having hollered. Over the edge of the bathtub emerged a white mug first, held by two hands, followed by arms and, at last, a face appeared in his field of vision.

"Oh, you are awake, that's good. Then it wasn't so bad", said the stranger without really stuttering and sat down on the edge of the tub turned towards him. He placed the steaming container he had brought on the narrow ridge of, so that it stood there rather dangerously unsteady. "How do you feel? Are you feeling better? Shall I get you to hospital to be on the safe side?"

He looked at him enquiringly without answering. They eyed each other, although without hostility. When their eyes met, the stranger shyly looked to the mug.

"I've made you tea to warm you from the inside." It seemed that the silence had made him feel awkward. Now that he had broken it, he looked at him with a good-natured, but hesitant smile.

"Cheers, I feel a little bit weak. I'll be okay soon", he replied, not to appear ungrateful. The other one softly pressed his lips together as a sign of comprehension and blinked briefly, took the cup with his left and leaned over the water, supporting himself with his right.

"You'll feel much better quickly." Assisting, the stranger held the tea to his mouth to let him drink. He opened his lips and a small sip ran down his throat and burned it. He wailed a short grunt. The stranger understood, took away the cup and leaned back into a more comfortable position.

"I'm sorry! I didn't consider that." He stammered again, looked down at him apologetically, then sat up with a jerk: " I think it's about time to get you out of the water. Too long isn't good, either." He put the mug down on the floor to the side. "Can you get up or shall I help you?"

He nodded slightly. With the stranger's energetic support he was manoeuvred out of the water and over the rim until he stood on the bath mat. He was still wearing nearly all his clothes, except his shoes and pullover, and therefore he dripped everything wet. The other one's jumper and jeans were affected as well.

"I will fetch you and me some dry clothes. Do sit down for a minute!"

Propped by the hand of the stranger he alighted on the edge of the tub and gazed after the stranger, who strode down the corridor and disappeared around the corner.

While he was waiting he was getting colder again. First he got goose-pimples, and then he started to shiver.

The stranger came back with a pile of clothes. As soon as he saw him he exclaimed: "Oh no, we have to get you out of your clothes as soon as possible."

He put the pile on the washing machine, pushing aside some of the items on it, and helped him to get undressed. Discreetly he turned around to grab one of the towels and, still turned away, to hand it over to him, while he undressed completely and toilsomely and put the towel around his waist. The young man took a large bath towel, helped him to stand up and towelled him down cautiously and scrupulously. He looked at him gratefully and sceptically at the same time, and wobbly held on to the wall and the open door.

When the stranger had finished, he stepped back and reached for the garments, but when he saw how the figure in front of him staggered, he swiftly pulled forth a long, fleecy bathrobe from behind the door and helped him to slip in, gave him a pair of thick socks and led him silently along the corridor into the living room, sat him down on the sofa and lay a snug blanket over his lap and shoulders. Then he left him alone again to get changed and bring the tea, which he put on the wooden table next to the sofa. Lastly, the stranger sank down in the armchair next to it and considered him attentively. They sat opposite each other. The stranger looked at him directly and unbashfully now.

He felt a bit better already and let his gaze browse through the living room without heeding the other one's look. He felt uncomfortable, because he felt terribly ashamed and was sure that the stranger expected some kind of explanation. He noticed that the dog was nowhere to be found. He conjectured that it was locked up in the bedroom. One of the doors was closed, when they had passed it. It was remarkable that he heard no barking, no howling, no scratching, no sound whatsoever. It was either a quiet animal in the house or it was sleeping. He asked the stranger, for he did not have to conceal his knowledge of the dog. The stranger confirmed that Ellie, which was the dog's name, slept in the bedroom.

The living room was quite small and lavishly furnished. The sofa, on which he sat, was fairly broad on the scale of things and it had rather high rests. It looked very old with its stuffy, brown and thick cover and did not fit to the design of the armchair next to it at all. He could gently feel the springs through the cushions, but still the sofa was very comfortable. Above it hung, in a golden, squiggly ornated frame, the oil-painted likeness of a pretty gypsy lady with a broad gold chain and a voluptuous red dress. To the left, between sofa and armchair, stood a life-size figure of a Nubian beauty with arms holding up a big ball, in which an opaque light shone. In front of the sofa stood a low, dark wooden table, which equally seemed to be out of fashion, but which looked precious with its handcrafted carvings and embellishments. On it several tealights burned in sundry holders and oozed atmosphere. Only one bigger object stood on the table: a huge crystal ball on a luxuriant wooden base. On the right of the sofa stood a light wooden rack replete with books, most of them doubtlessly antiquities, a few videos, a huge collection of vinyl and an audio equipment with a record player. The door next to the rack led to the corridor and the remaining rooms of the flat. Straight ahead of him stood a bulgy chest of drawers in a rather baroque style with a bulky television set on top, and left of it a huge weeping fig. On the right side of the commode the room was somewhat deeper forming a recess for a dinette of three red chairs and a simple table, which was pushed to the wall. On top of it lay a few magazines and stood a vintage cash register. A door in the wall left of the niche opened to a tiny kitchen, which stretched out behind the wall behind the telly. A bulb in a papery round shade with darker ribs of wire hung from the ceiling in the middle of the living room, whereas a lamp of purple glass in Sixties style loomed over the dining nook. Both lamps were switched off.

The furnishing was an omnium-gatherum of the quaintest pieces, not merely a motley collection of inexpensive and accumulated furnishings, but authentic, precious objects which he did not expected in the young man's place. He was smitten with amazement and wondered where all these things might have come from. Were they heirloom?

On the window ledge to the left were lush plants, which flourished and blossomed in defiance of the season. A glass door next to the window led to a small balcony, on which a few strong plants braved the autumn weather. Darkness had spread across the world beyond. The wind screeched around the corner of the house eerily, but it could not touch them here. Here they were protected. He felt safe.

Found Me

You have found me
and don't know me at all.
You will wound me,
ere my heart starts to talk.

We are facing each other,
close to each other stand we.
You look straight in my face,
but you don't recognise me.

You cannot come close.
Myself I'll conceal.
Forgotten tomorrow,
as if I've never been real.

You have forgot me.
I have not been real.
Remembrance did flee.
I am under seal.

What sense did it make
that you have found me?
For shadow I am.
Oblivion's my plea.

6

He had completed his visual expedition through this foreign territory and was noticeably impressed. He leaned forward, held the blanket at the hemline, so that it did not slide from his nap, and reached out to grab the mug. He leaned back and took a swig. There was honey and quite a twist of lemon in the tea making it taste refreshingly sweet-sour. He put his hands with the container on his lap and looked at the stranger, who was still beholding him. The other one's face was beaming with a certain pride in the furnishing, but out of contradictory modesty he did not ask him how he liked it.

They were looking at each other wordlessly, without avoiding each other's gaze, although the silence was awkward. A thousand questions probably weighed heavily on the other's mind, but he did not ask one, containing himself out of tact and contenting himself with his knowledge of human nature and presuppositions until he would dare to ask. Both of them had their assumptions and explanations in regard to the one opposite and his story. This had to suffice for the time being. None of them said a word to break the silence. Both wanted to learn more about the other one, but neither dared to break the ice, because in the end the respective other was a stranger. On the other hand, he was very clear on the fact that the stranger had helped him, had apparently carried him hither. And the situation in the bathroom could well have been described as intimate, at least by his standards. Nevertheless, or maybe because of this, their bashfulness and reservation concerning social contact with other people predominated. Perhaps the stranger had once been bitten too. Anyway, this messed-up situation hardly offered any ground to get to know each other in a simple way. The incidence in the forest had been mysterious and disturbing. To start a conversation without talking about this seemed to be impossible and inappropriate; both of them felt this. Yet to talk about it would have been most exceedingly disconcerting. It demanded embarrassing explications, which the stranger did not want to wrest from him, not if it did not come unsolicited.

The stranger went into the kitchen and got himself a mug as well. He brought the whole pot and filled up both cups. The tea steamed and little clouds of vapour rose up swirling. He went over to the rack, took something from it and turned towards the other one, who was watching what the stranger did.

"Would you like to watch a movie?" asked the stranger breaking the silence with nervous stutter. He wanted to distract him somehow from the awkwardness, to entertain him if they did not converse. "I have, for example, Carter's first film ever, if you are interested."

"I already know it, but why not? I could watch it over and over again. It is and will remain one of his best."

The covert broad hint did not escape him in any way: So he remembered their meeting in the cinema. There was no use in denying. How much more did the stranger know about him? He had to be more cautious from now on not to let him know too much about himself and not to let him come too close. For the first time ever he had the impression that someone could be a menace to him in this respect.

"Alright then", said the stranger and opened one of the drawers in which the video was stored away cunningly. It was a top loader, a really old model. He wondered how the cables ran and where he had this old dearie from. That it was still functioning! The other one reached for the remote control, which was lying on the television set, and sat down on the sofa next to him, because the view was much better from there—though not as great as the cinema. The TV was tuned in on the right channel and the film was started.

"I think it's better if I switch off Molly", the stranger grinned impishly, stoop up once again and operated the switch of the cable leading across the floor from the plug under the window up to the Nubian lady lamp.

"Her name is Molly?" he asked incredulously.

The stranger nodded: "My grandmother used to get a kick out of making fun of it." The smirk on his face got even wider. He sat down again, blew out half of the candles and leaned back to watch the film.

Thus they sat next to each other. Their gazes were directed to the video screen in front of them, but their attention was turned to each other mostly. It was absurd. Both were sitting tensed up, tried to move as little as possible. Although the film was excruciatingly funny, they both suppressed their laughter not to bother the other one. They could have been sitting next to each other dead, it would not have changed a thing, he thought to himself and grasped the macabre side to his thoughts. Afterwards he was even stiller.

In the meantime things were livened up only once when cunning Ellie opened the bedroom door by herself and greeted the unfamiliar visitor bow-wowing and wagging the tail. He reacted rather displeased at the attack of the animal, but Ellie did not readily let up on him. At the stranger's recommendation he petted her behind the ear shortly with some self-conquest, which seemed to becalm her. At last it lay down in front of the chest and only roamed about the flat every now and then, toddling loudly on the laminate floor with its paws.

Only three tealights were still burning on the table. The film was over and they had not exchanged a single word during the whole time, except for when the dog came in. One could have got the impression that these two were dumb. The stranger reached for the remote control, switched off the TV, stopped the video and rewound the tape.

He looked around for a clock, but he could not find a single one in the entire room, not even on the VCR. He was puzzled, for he had in fact expected that everybody had at least one clock in a living room. Had he overlooked it? He eyed around once again, but again remained unsuccessful this second time. At last he turned to the stranger next to him, who had grasped his mug and had emptied it in one thirsty gulp.

"Can you tell me how late it is?"

"One moment please", replied the stranger, reached for the remote, which he had put aside, turned on the TV again and opened the teletext. Both could plainly read it, which is why the other one saved the labour to read it out aloud in answer. By this time it was shortly after ten. The film had quite some overlength.

"I think it's about time for me to leave", he declared without explanation in order to be start leaving. On a Friday night his mother should already lie in bed fast asleep at this time, because she was totally overwrought from work. She seemed to trust in his own responsibility and had never waited up worried about him. It was simply too odd for him to stay at the strangers and to keep on bearing the silence. Not that he was categorically against silence, but it was completely different and weird, if someone unknown was sitting next to you and one could downright feel the unspoken expectations billowing in the room.

"I don't know if it's such a good idea to go out alone at night before All Hallows. It is an ominous and dangerous time", declared the stranger his misgiving. He seemed somewhat disquieted, but surprisingly he did not stutter.

"Oh, humbug! I don't live that far away and it's not even close to midnight. What's more, only Americans celebrate Halloween", he objected. That he did not live far away was surely nothing new for the young man, thus he said it without the slightest qualm.

Ignoring this completely, the stranger replied softly: "Probably you are right. Sometimes I am just way too superstitious."

They both stood up. He felt significantly better. He put aside the blanket. Only now that he stood it came back to his mind that he was still wearing nothing but the bathrobe. The other one noticed that as well.

"There are dry clothes for you in the bath. I hope they're not far too big for you."

The bloke sat down again, while he left the living room. The dog lumbered a few steps behind him, but stopped at the threshold to the corridor and let him go to the bathroom alone, where he dressed leisurely. The stranger's clothes were pretty large indeed and hung around his slight body like sacks. The stuff was comfortable, by no means fashionable and made of rather plain or coarse fabric. That the clothes were quite baggy would have made them more comfortable, had they not been so large. He rolled up the sleeves and trousers, gathered his wet clothes, wrung them out in the tub and wadded them up to a bundle, which he carried out of the bathroom on his left arm.

The stranger sat in the armchair. He had replaced the burned-out tealights and lit all of them anew. On the table in front of him were placed two small, gold-ornamented glasses and a brandy flask made of clay, which was unlabelled.

"This is an old tradition of ours to drink on this occasion, so put aside your stuff and drink with me!"

He did as he was told, even if he was wearing a sceptical frown, and came into the living room. The stranger took the bottle, opened it somewhat heavy-handedly and filled the glasses. One of these he handed over to him and he accepted it.

"This night was the night before the new year of the pagans, for example the Celts or the Saxons, a kind of ancient New Year's Eve, which had been celebrated with fire festivities to drive off evil spirits. The pagans also believed that the souls of the departed returned to their old homes. Sometimes even the dark forces were invoked to make prophecies about weddings, luck, health or death. Let's drink to our good luck!"

They raised their glasses together, he raised a cheers and they clinked their glasses. Secretly he had drunk to his only suspended death with himself, without the stranger's know-ledge. When he brought the glass to his lips, he was able to smell the strong flavour of fruit, herbs and alcohol of the dark schnapps. He inhaled it deeply and swigged the drop down his gorge. It burned terribly and he was feeling hot. He gave a little cough and felt how the devilish brewage flushed down towards his stomach and set it on fire too. The stranger blew out fiery breath agonised. After a troublesome moment the stranger spontaneously grinned at him suddenly, as if they were conspiring together. He replied an overcome, shy smile.

"What was that?"

"Elder liqueur."

"Thank you! I have to go now", he said and put the shot glass back on the table. Normally it was very difficult for him to proffer his thanks, unless it was for a trifle. He regarded his thanks to be motivated by the drink, but he hoped that the young man related it rather to the whole evening.

"It was nothing!" The stranger grew graver, put his glass next to the other and ushered his guest to the door, which he unlocked and opened with the advice to take in a lot of vitamin C and to keep warm.

"And don't forget your backpack", he had to remind him and the situation turned disconcerting once again. Ellie pranced about in the corridor and tried to say goodnight to the visitor by licking his left hand. He pulled it away, turned around and shouldered his damp bag, which stood in the corner, picked up the bundle of wet clothes from the floor and stepped through the door. Without another word, only with a simple, trivial nod he went to the stairs with lowered head and lifted his eyes only for a last shy glance. When he had reached the first landing, the stranger called out an enquiry after his name and stepped forward in anticipation to see him squint around the corner once again.

"Wulf", it sounded up the staircase, while his footfalls clattered down the steps. Before the stranger could tell his name in reply, Wulf had already vanished through the front door out into the night.

The stranger went back into the flat, closed the door and sank down in his armchair lost in thought.

Depressive

I discovered a scar upon my breast,
have tasted my injured heart's blood.
For my harm's origin I now quest,
the well of this mighty fatal flood.

Behind the seeming fortune
I've discovered plain bad luck
which bears me down until I swoon.
This feeling is a frosty hell.
Without a feel, my heart is cold,
and I in fear the rest withhold.
I fight with sarcasm and irony.
If someone comes close, I have to flee.
I must watch humanity croak.
I'm afraid my soul will never be well.

'Cause people could hurt me again,
I left my heart's path ne'er exposed.
I could not cherish any joy enclosed.
So I'd replace it with the wonted pain,
for bliss devoid of sentience has no gain.

I'd leave every delightful bed,
just because I feel unworthy.
Again I'd wish a hero rescued me,
but if a saviour came, he'd seem a dread.

Deep in me rage contrasts hard to wield,
not even I know my heart's need.
But my aplomb is then indeed
my most important treasure sealed.

The question is where and when I'll find it.
Maybe when I leave this gloomy dale
through which I since so long travail;
maybe when I start to kind it;
after recognizing bit by bit
what to myself I never did admit.

I have to change the leopard's spots,
for the secret that I did evade
can only unravel my life's knots,
since my heart's feelings had decayed.

So this will be a complicated quest,
for who is able to tell where t'is writ
into my book of life depressed.
If it was up to mischief tightly knit,
'cause it was writ in the prologue of it
that I would never learn myself to love,
then every toil was totally in vain
because I couldn't change what I'm made of.
Giving in to the temptation's reign
I can only tell nothing is well.

7

The stranger did not hear from Wulf for days. He went for a walk, but neither in the street, in the forest nor at the oak did he come across him. These were sombre, grey, cold days. It rained virtually without ceasing, seldom did the rain turn into a light drizzle. The thick cloud cover did not lift once. The few people that the stranger saw in the street wore their coats high-necked, collars turned up and their faces stony. They hurried on the pavement like sad harlequins and sidestepped great puddles. Colourful umbrellas fought against the storm and clearly lost against the general autumn melancholy, which had also seized the stranger. The noose dangled in the wind on one of the oak's boughs, and soon it would be its only jewellery, for bit by bit did the wind bereave the tree of its withered leaves. Still it was covered with foliage. Nobody had discovered it yet.

The stranger sat home a lot in his armchair, drank herbal tea by the light of many candles, lost in his autumn reading or in thought, his gaze focused on one of the flickering flames. He thought much about the encounter with Wulf, whether it had changed him in any way and whether he thought about him too. He wondered what had hurled him into desperation so deep that he ran through the forest in the cold autumn without heeding the weather. Did he not deliberate that he could have caught his death? He made conjectures what might have happened in his life or must have gone wrong that he cared so little about his health.

The stranger was patient. He knew that he couldn't force a person like Wulf to make a contact. Yes, he knew such characters which were weary of life and did not let anyone come close to them, and he knew about a lot full of anguish, which some people had drawn. In addition he was a little shy himself. Besides, he did not know how to find him. He would have to come of his own accord. Patience was one of the stranger's virtues. Yet every day his concern grew that he was miserable or that he might have harmed himself. Then their encounter had only postponed the inevitable. The stranger did not want to make friends with this thought, for he hoped that the slight hypothermia and their acquaintance might have purified him to some degree.

After four days the door rang in the late afternoon. Ellie came running from her feeding dish in the kitchen. After the stranger had opened the door, he came up the stairs with careful steps. He was dressed in black like every time he had seen him before. Raindrops sparkled on his leather jacket in the hall light like black diamonds. The dog welcomed him hoydenishly and wanted to be fondled. The stranger was profoundly relieved and pleased to see him here, but could not assess how readily the visitor had actually come or if he merely felt obliged. They looked at each other with unmoved miens, concerned about dissembling their thoughts.

In a plastic bag, to keep them safe from the rain, he had brought the borrowed clothes. He stayed at the door and handed them over to the stranger. They were freshly washed but not ironed, he said. The stranger didn't even deign a peek into the bag. It was a matter of complete indifference to him in which condition the togs were or that he had brought them at all. He would not even have cared one tiny bit if he had kept them or had thrown them away. Such things were easy to replace. To him other things were much more important, for example the fact that Wulf had come back.

"Are you alright? No flu or so?", the stranger enquired after him stammering and asked his guest to come in.

"I had a mild sniffle, but with a lot of vitamin C, as you had advised me, it went away quite quickly", he reported unusually talkative and followed his invitation. The dog in turn followed the two. The shoes which were soaking wet he left on the mat at the sill to the flat. He hung his jacket on a hook behind the door, which the stranger closed behind him. Together they went into the living room. It was odd how relatively trite and familiar and at the same time standoffish the reception had been.

"Are you hungry or thirsty? Can I offer you anything?" the stranger asked after him, so as not to forget his manners. He was a bit bashful and stuttered mildly.

"Something to drink would be nice."

"What would you like then? I'd have something very special. Would you like to try it?"

"Well, I don't really know. But why not?" he said casually and sat down on the sofa, while the stranger shuffled into the kitchen and the dog flounced around the dwelling. He looked at the dinette. He felt strangely lonely. He did not have any explanation for it, for he was constantly alone and used to it. It was probably an inexplicable thrust of realisation of his desolation in the company of a friendly being. It was as if the life in him flared up a last time in sheer desperation in order to send a Save Our Souls to the people around. It was a tremendous, a horrendous feeling. His eyes were flooded. He felt it and recognised it by the well-known blurring of his sight. He hoped that the other one did not notice.

The young man sat down next to him with two beakers in his hands and gave one of them to him. He took it and glanced into it. In it was a deeply purple liquid, somewhat viscous, almost creamy. It smelled sweetish and fruity.

"What is it?"

"Elderberry juice."

"Did you make it yourself?"

"Yes, I still have my mother's old juicer. In the past we used to make it together. She even made jam and liqueur out of it, but she never showed me how to make it."

"Where is she now?" he asked as cautiously as he could, for he had sensed that this was a topic which would stir up sentimentality.

"She passed a few years ago. I don't have much of her liqueur left, but I make the juice myself every autumn to remember them and to get over this darksome season", the stranger explicated and threw a stealthy, undetected peep to the painting over the couch.

He nodded sympathetically and looked into his cup, the content of which appeared to be more valuable and profound all of a sudden. He brought the beaker to his mouth and tried the juice. It was a bit mealy, sweet, with a whiff of bitterness. After the first mouthful he understood better why this was the stranger's autumn salvation. He felt the consoling comfort which the drink bestowed. At least there was some solace in the world.

The autumn was nasty. It was dismally grey, the thick blanket of clouds swallowed all the light and the trees tottered in the storm, embarrassed of their nakedness. They sang a sad song to which one better not listened. It made souls sore and tired, tired of living.

Against an outside world so hostile towards life, one had to shut oneself away vigorously in the privacy of one's home. The stranger presumably had many talents, even if these were undiscovered hitherto. One of them, which was obvious even to him, was to create a cosy atmosphere: warming, snug, wholesome. The drink was just one of his measures. Many a candle flickered again. They were distributed all over the place and exuded their orange light in this well-tempered room. The turntable spinned Soul classics, the rhythms of which were blithe, melodies were jovial and vocals sounded serene and warm. They were the sunshine for a sickly soul.

A mood like the one he encountered here he had never got to know. It alarmed him suddenly, when he noticed how much it had soothed him within. The music was absolutely not his cup of tea and homely places usually released a pulse in him to take flight. It was most strange.

Subsequently the two young men had a talk about everything under the sun, although without getting all too personal. They were insecure, albeit for different reasons, and yet both desired in secret to learn more about the other one.

He did not stay long. As much as he savoured the peacefulness in the stranger's dwelling, his fear of people got the better of him after some time and drove him out into the inhospitable autumn reality. Above all he must never have peace, he recalled to his attention, as he betook himself into the cold evening after the farewell. Except in his grave! He was forgetting his obligation, he scolded himself and embraced the strong wind. He did not go home yet but roved through the sombreness in order to do penance.

However, he visited the stranger again after a few days, this time longer.

Standard Colours

My trousers and my shirt.
My eyes, my face and even my thoughts.
The car passing by and the driver.
The dog on the lead and the old lady.
The food I ingested for lunch.
The home I walk past.
The sky and its cloud ceiling.

The chilly rain dripping on the asphalt.
The trees wind-shaken.
My hand at the umbrella.

Autumn celebrates its coming.
Even the stars dictate grey.

Only a young woman under a rainbow umbrella
defies the regime with a brilliant rose smile.

8

The stranger or the other one, this is what I was for him and this is how he referred to me, even if not in my face, yet still in his thoughts and writings, in which he was very frank and private. That Wulf called me the stranger was due to his peculiar personality. He had probably never acknowledged that a first blush of friendship between us was starting to show, and therefore he cheated himself with these phrasings. He was a lone wolf and did not have any friends. He did not permit himself any for some reason or another. He did not disclose much about himself, and most of the time he remained vague when I asked him something personal inadvertently, though sometimes also advisedly. He was constantly on the guard, suspicious as if he was on the run, as if he was hunted by someone or something. I never saw him truly eased or happy.

The stranger he called me, and yet in fact he remained the stranger to me as to everyone else. That he gave me his name was a great present of his. It almost appeared as if his name was the key to his soul, to which no one was to be granted access. Nevertheless, he had transiently endowed me with it. Maybe he had done this in the hope that fleetingness stole back his name. However much I opened and told myself to him, he remained introverted and secretive. He had a marked tendency towards depressiveness, as if something forbid him to enjoy life. Sometimes I had the impression to be able to see how a shy smile in the corners of his mouth was washed away by a flood wave of fear and guilt. He hid himself from life. His shyness, cautiousness, negativity and scepticism, they had cast a dark veil over his appearance. Incessantly he exercised in unnatural non-commitment. Continually he was captured by an atrabilious mood, which surrounded him like a grey cloud, an aura of fear. As hopeless as it seemed, I steadily looked behind it, deep into his inside, and saw an immortal spark, a passion to live, which was never extinguished. To this I addressed my appeal. I fed my hope with his always elusive sight to break his dark spell. The further November progressed, the stronger my hope grew to succeed.

The stranger I was to him, and yet his friend. His only. Nobody knew anything about his character, not even his own mother knew him more than rudimentally. I surmise that some people in his environment, for example his school, had passed hasty judgements on him without going to the trouble of seeing behind the curtain. Therefore it is now my endeavour to tell his story. There is nobody else who could. But it must be done, this the voice of my heart asks of me. I have to tell Wulf's story, although the voice of my mind tells me that I am not a good storyteller. My destiny has brought me into this position, which is why I must vanquish the critic that I am myself. I am not a Shakespeare, Goethe, Rilke or a Molière, who knows how to wield words eloquently. I am just a simple man, who finds himself in this unavoidable position and has to face his fate bravely. May my grammatical and intellectual awkwardness be forgiven!

Wulf's life was singular, his story sad. Something was unutterable; something had gone disturbingly wrong and had mutilated him inside in the extreme. To reconstruct this though, I am lacking significant details which would join the pieces of this puzzle together. But what I know and what I conjecture I have tried to compile in order to illuminate Wulf's fate the best that I can. I devoutly hope that I will do justice to his spirit.

He was a good person, in my view even a very special one, a strong one. He would not harm a fly, had a sensitive intuition about the moods of other people, as well as manners and a sincere modesty. He was fond of telling tales, especially in a written form, although he was deeply convinced that it was not worthwhile to talk about himself, for he deemed his own story insignificant and boring. He was fond of listening to enrich his stock of anecdotes which he might put down in writing some time. Even pleading, begging or torturing, one could not get a single word out of him about himself, which is why I never leaned on him for it. Only in his secret poems he got personal, which might be the reason why he even placed them above his life.

Apart from them his life did not mean anything to him, that much is clear. His loneliness amounted to life imprisonment and raised the question what he was done for. He himself must have been the accused, defence lawyer, the biased prosecutor and judge in his trial, all at the same time. This fourfold role allocation must have frazzled him horridly. Which human being, except a very strong personality, can survive the pressure of such a process, convinced and confirmed in his sentence, without his indignant soul taking a vital knock? He must have incurred the guilt of a vast wrong, an overwhelming guilt, which notwithstanding did not destroy him completely, but which amazingly enough impelled him and made him gain strength. But his indispensible guilt did not press for a sentence of instanteneous death, which could have been pronounced all the same. Was the measureless penitence of a mindless vegetating to be preferred over the immediate forfeiture of his life? Quite evidently so! To die was not appropriate for his guiltiness. Therefore he was in debt for his life and a form of compensatory atonement, an expiation for life.

I cannot understand why any person would condemn themselves to isolation. From experience I know that quite many people are suffering from loneliness unjustly, wishing for nothing more profoundly than a companion, who they absolutely cannot find. It may well be that these people are not causelessly alone, even if their cause might be arcane or lost to them. Fundamentally nothing is ever causeless, but we shy away from the consequences, afraid of the responsibility to retrieve the reason and to eliminate it. I have never, until I came to know Wulf, known anyone in person who had chosen this kind of self-punishment on his own free will and in full consciousness. I am sure that a further aspect appertained to Wulf's guiltiness, something that actually replaced his will to survive, pushed him further and forbade him to give up, an aim that he clearly kept in mind and pursued, a task that needed to be taken care of, even if it had been held back from me so far. Maybe I will identify more of his delinquency, his punishment and his duty in the further course of the story that I am obligated to tell.

The stranger he called me, and therefore I call it myself here, for I am telling this story for him and from his perspective. Who the stranger really was to whom I can hardly tell myself anymore, after I have brought myself so deep into his point of view. On my short quest with him I was afraid sometimes that I would lose myself for all the strangeness. But who stepped through the deepest vale knows to appreciate the highest mountain. For that reason I hope that he, the ever nameless, has in the silence found a name, that he, the lone Wulf, has in his solitude found a faithful companion, and that he, the one with the black doleful heart, has in his deepest darkness found the brightest light.

…Without Sense

What's the point in walking?
The aim seems beyond reach.
What's the point in seeking?
Never will I find it.

What's the point of hoping,
but admitting there is lack?
What's the point of trusting,
if nobody entrusts to me?

Does it make sense to pray
that broken glass fixes itself?
Does it make sense to know,
when the grey matter's mortal?

Why do I reason?
Why am I being hurt?
Why do I try to love
if no one understands me anyway?

What's the point of our striving forward?
What's the point of feelings?
Is there any sense at all
or is everything we do in vain?

Is life fate or coincidence?
Are we simply here by chance?
...Without sense?

9

He had spent the last week primarily with going to school and learning. The weather had cleared up for only one day and he had used that day to roam the clime. He did not feel like going to the oak at the moment and he did not want to visit the stranger too often, after all not only the other one had better things to do. He too should attend to more important things than friendship. He had to be extremely careful that he did not let it become a habit, or else it could well be that he broke his resolution.

School was tedious, but it was no use. So he sat down and swotted, did his written homework thoroughly and prepared texts. He also finished reading his Hamlet during schooltime. Again he was only met with indifference from his fellow pupils, provided that one could talk about meeting at all. They treated him like a nothing and did not even make a joke out of making fun of him or despising him. Every once in a while Mr Angerman gave him looks filled with fervent aversion but left him alone for the time being. If school had not been hell, this indifference could almost have been heaven.

It was a mystery to him why teachers like Angerman and all the others were allowed to teach. Who decided that they were psychologically qualified for the handling of children? They only rattled off their curriculum without ever caring whether the pupils comprehended it, reciting it down like an Our Father. Many treated their pupils contemptuously, as if the pupils in front of them were no rational young beings. And he started to marvel about the teachers' pedagogical and empathetic incapability. Not once had a member of the teaching staff, not even the form mistress, taken him aside and had a talk with him. Not once!

None of the adults seemed to understand his position in the class or his humour, much less to react to it. He was convinced that, had he been a teacher, he had shown considerably more sensitivity and had lent his support for his pupils' good as much as he could. He surely had also supported somebody like himself and had tried to help him.

This was an odd thought, he figured. Why would he help himself if he were a teacher, and did not in effect help himself out of the situation which he was in? What's more, this train of thoughts made it look natural that someone like him needed help and was not allowed to stay in these circumstances. Was melancholy an illness? Were there pills against lonerism or a lack of social life? What would a psychologist have do, after he had talked to him? Prescribed him an antidepressant or lithium? Sent him to psychotherapy to recover from school abuse, or even sectioned him? He really wasn't a lunatic. And he was convinced that no psychologist would ever have noticed what was truly going on inside of him and which circumstances moulded him, if he didn't have wanted it. Nobody could muster up that much empathy, and surely he would have known which answers were desirable and which marked someone down as maladjusted in psychological tests. Since he had all his wits about him, he would have said what they wanted to hear in such a situation, and nobody would have discovered him.

Anyhow, all at once he wondered vehemently, if he really was as sensible as he envisioned himself to be. Or was he nothing more than a nutcase in reality?

But then again, never before had one single person indicated that they cared or sympathised. Never had there been anyone who had taken a sincere interest in his person or his problems, his thoughts and his being. Never had there been one single person around whom he had felt at ease and safe with, until this outlandish stranger had crossed his path and had sneaked up on him lead by his dog. Unerringly the stranger had stormed his allegedly secure bastion of seclusion. From now on there was no more safety in his life and he was faced with the decision whether he let the invader move into his stronghold or whether he had to flee from it into nothingness in order to stay true to himself.

Most of the time he spent with brooding over this question, staring into the dull clouds and going astray in saturnine thoughts. The world had become so insecure that he did not know where to turn to, where to hide away. He did not even dare to trust his soul, for it allowed this stranger with more and more joy to become important to it. Who was this individual, that he threatened to destroy his whole world view, his world construct, so swiftly? Who was he, that he let himself be unsettled to that degree by an imaginary soul that wanted to bind him to another human against his own decision to be forlorn? What kind of connection did his soul have to him, that on the one hand he trusted its advice for some incomprehensible reason and wanted to comply with its wishes, and on the other hand mistrusted it and held it in contempt? Why did he not trust his feelings, his voice inside, and surceased from his long-cherished grief, from his sadness, his eternal, friendly pain?

Who or what was his soul anyway? This was the big question which he had to clarify once and for all. What was the soul to him and what kind of relationship did he bear to it? Was there a soul in the first place or was it only a construct of his biochemical perception? Accompanying this, were souls immortal or did they extinguish together with the last sparks of thought? If what he was taught to call soul was nothing more than a mental illusion, why did he agonise himself with the yearning for these romantic feelings and values of friendship? Why then did he feel so helpless against the power of his own illusions? If however the soul was this spiritual, eternal part of his self, the essential part of that which he called his self, why did he then fight himself? All the while he must have become untrue to his souls, ergo his self, in the first place, and this he had not.

These and similar thoughts haunted him during these days and insisted on clarification, because the subsequent certainty hankered for a decision. A very vital decision! For the quintessence of all these questions, the quintquestion so to speak, was if that which he described as soul, whatever that was in the end, tried to set him on the wrong track or to get him back on the straight and narrow. He was certain that this temptation was an affliction. He wrote that word down because it was a strange word. He looked it up in a dictionary and it said that affliction literally meant to have been struck down. That was true enough, he had been struck down by his fate. But then again what was fate? The dictionary stated that it originated from things spoken. Who commanded the predetermination? Was it God, his soul, he himself or really only chance? Surely it wasn't biochemistry which predetermine fateful events. But how well meant either of these entities? Was it their call to grow or was it just a blow?

He seemed determined to go to any length to get answers to his questions and find out which the truth in the end was. He reckoned that all these thoughts were just illusions of the brain and that he returned to nothingness. But from which primordial ground had life and consciousness then sprouted? From chance?

Self-Forgotten Angel

At last detach yourself from this crude world
with all its ardent longing and its pain,

which keeps your wings from being unfurled,
from your striving upwards to God's plane.

It holds you back with its carnality.
Still long's the path which leads up to the good,
which leads up to diviner light and glee,
to heavenly bless'dness and sainthood.

For the moment your days are numbered here.
Hearken! You've been summoned home by God.
For you're expected in the highest sphere,
don't dally in your self-forgotten trot.

Abandon us and go play with your sort
instead of giving yourself up for dreams.
You'll make it back into this earthly port,
but until then you'll live with the Supreme.

Your being's soaring up into the sky,
into the peaceful kingdom of God's heaven,
where everyone's floating mentally high,
light as air, quick as thought, like in a sweven.

Bethink yourself of your angelic nature,
of the empyrean creature that you are.
Don't feign that ever you had human stature,
and leave, ere your self's forgotten, angel-star!

10

After a couple of days he stood at the stranger's door again. It was a Friday afternoon and he expected the other one to be off. He hesitated to ring the bell. With every step, however small it may be, towards the stranger he drifted farther away from his anguish. How far still was he allowed to go until there was no return? How far still before he had crossed the threshold to betraying himself? How far ere he had broken his vow? Every time he became more and more careful, deliberate and hesitant, for he had pledged his troth to the pain. He was bound until death parted them, he thought fiercely. And yet something else inside of him became more alert and livelier and stronger. He was horrified to realise that he had rung already.

The door opener buzzed. He entered the hallway, which was sheltered from the wind and the rain, and climbed the stairs. The dog came down to meet him at half a flight. With utmost satisfaction he noticed that he still didn't like the dog. He had not forgiven the animal, because it bore the blame that he was in contact with this human and did not know how to deal with it now. The stranger stood in the door and watched closely how he tried to get rid of the dog.

"Ellie!" the other one admonished and she obeyed his every word, let go of him and returned to her master. He eased his cramped posture when he looked up to the stranger and thanked him.

"Nice to see you again. Do come in!"

The stranger took his coat and hung it on a hook, while he took off his shoes at the door. He went into the living room, where the dog was already sitting and waiting in front of the sofa. A loud whistling resounded from the kitchen.

"Oh, that's the tea kettle", said the stranger behind him and pushed his way past him. "You came just in time."

He followed a few steps, but stayed at the kitchen door and watched how the other one brewed the tea, gathered a pair of spoons and big cups, a sugar basin and a jug of milk upon the tray on which the tea was already placed and which he lifted up. He made room for him and followed him to the sofa. The other one put down the tray on the living-room table, climbed over the dog and sat down.

"Are you up for a game?" he was asked, while he was making himself comfortable. Without really waiting for his answer, the other one got up and climbed over the dog once again and brought a wooden box from one of the drawers of the chest. Sitting down again he placed the box on his lap, shoved the tray with his left arm farther away on the table and opened the casket. Therein were ebony and ivory chess pieces, carefully stored in velvety depressions especially designed for them, and a board panelled with ebony and ivory fields and hinged in the middle.

The other one placed the opened game on the table and hereafter pressed the box with the pieces into his hands. While he was busy turning the pieces between his fingers, beholding minutely the skilful details and arranging them one after another on the board, the other one took the teabag out of the pot, poured the steaming beverage into the cups and filled them up with fresh full-cream milk. The stranger also offered him rock sugar, but he declined. The other one put a spoonful of sugar into his own cup and stirred it chinkingly.

"Where did you in fact get all that stuff from?" he asked the other one. "Many of the things that you have look old, as if they have been bequeathed to you, and yet they seem so motley."

The young man kindly prompted him to open the game. After his first move the other one started to answer his question, and like the game evolved with every move, their conversation built up more and more. Above all the other one talked about himself, about his life, about his past. He didn't have to ask more questions but simply listened to his opposite with astonished wonder and binding interest.

The wedding of the stranger's parents had not been received well by both families. His father came from a tradition-steeped industrialist family, his mother was a gypsy, but they loved each other. Both sides of the family were so displeased with this union that they broke ties with their respective children independently of each other. Only his mother's mother had attended to her grandson's interests, albeit clandestinely, had visited him and his mother once and again when she could, or had sent presents. Some time later did the heart of his grandfather on his father's side soften a little, after his wife had died, but all too soon had the widower followed his wife. After the grandparents on both sides had died, his parents' siblings had snaffled the greatest part of the heritage and left his parents only a few disagreeable curios. A couple of years ago his mother had died of cancer and shortly after his father of grief, so that he had assembled his own smaller flat with the motley huddle of furnishings and fittings. The stranger had tried to keep what was nicest and most significant to him, but he lacked the space for quite a few things in this rather restricted flat. He had sold a part of the furniture, saved the money, lived frugally on a part-time job and deliberated on where and how he should take a chance on a fresh start.

The stranger had had a difficult time during school, for he had been teased, ostracised or even beaten. They simply did not like him because he was a half-breed in their eyes. He did not feel that he really belonged anywhere, since nobody accepted him as who he was. In the pretty small and decent village where he came from not far from here, each and everyone just saw that he did not belong to them, for his looks were a little different. Even his mother's clan, had he known where they were, might not have regarded him as one of their kin, as he suspected. It was an abominable situation, for he could not change who he was. He had dropped out of school early and found a carpenter, with who he was able to train and who could not have cared less about whether his hair was frizzy or how bad he stammered after these terrible years at school.

After his parents' death he had packed up his stuff and had turned his back on this narrow-minded village in order to try his luck in the next larger city. But he didn't warm to this town yet and therefore longed to go away. Away was no distinct direction though, and every place was tolerable with Ellie, so he stayed until he had found a better destination.

He listened spellbound, for he was surprised that the stranger could talk about his life and tale of woe so precisely and frankly, whereas he never wanted to talk about himself. Furthermore it confounded him how similar their odd fates seemed to be, although there was a big difference between them: He had chosen his withdrawal wilfully, while the other one was the involuntary victim of his circumstances.

He listened intrigued and pondered at the same time. He believed that the other one would surely have been discrete and understanding, if he had talked about himself. Nevertheless he didn't have the nerve to do that. Nobody was as reserved and diffident as he was, and he had to be careful not to give in to the temptation to build sympathy on the cheap basis of similar life situations. But he did not want or need to have friends nor was he allowed to. In spite of that he spent time with the stranger now and again.

While the game continued, the stranger particularised some other experiences and occurrences. Although he had been listening carefully all the time, he had not noticed that the other one had cast off his stutter completely. And he did not notice at all that the young man had begun to blossom in some respects over the last weeks, because he didn't know how the stranger had been until recently. He was only partly aware that he had begun to change as well, but this he was fighting. That at the end of the game, which he won, he was beaming with joy and pride was something he was not cognizant of, for example. The stranger however did not fail to notice it.

Thornbush

The thornbush stood alone
and felt awfully lonesome.
Therefore it set off to find another
just as lonesome unwillingly.
It really searched everywhere
and tried mightily,
and although it met like-minded ones,
the right one wasn't among them.
It did not understand why those
that it was attracted to
shrinked from it, avoided it;
in turn the disagreeable
and repulsive pestered it.
The only thing it grasped were
that the disagreeable had thorns
which were longer and spikier than its own.

11

A week later at school he was the last one to leave the classroom for break. At first he had wanted to eat his sandwich there, but then he had changed his mind yet again. He went left along the hallway which led to the spacious main staircase which was quiet except for a few hurried pupils. The sky had broken open this morning, a little bit of sun shone through the clouds and the teachers had sent all pupils out into the schoolyard, so that they stayed outside once again after these long weeks of rain. Only those in the sixth form were allowed to stay in the building at their own will. He sat down on the cool marble of the great staircase and bit in his sandwich, which his mother had made for him although he always indicted that he could make one himself. Lost in thought he gnawed on it and stared straight down the stairs into space.

Without him taking heed of it, the door to the toilettes behind him opened and Caroline went out. She smoothed out her blouse, approached him from behind with the marked clicking of heels and cleared her throat to demand his attention. He started slightly and turned around to her expecting to see one of the teachers, who wanted to urge him to go out as well. Astonishment mingled to his aversion to Caroline and a pinch of curiosity what she might be up to.

"Hey, what's doing?" she addressed him casually, and what he wanted most was to beat this manner of expression out of her head. Maybe this was the simple reason that he did not belong to them, that he was the odd one out. Without responding to her he turned back around, rested his head with his elbow upon his knee and munched on his sandwich. Caroline sat down next to him and looked at him cheekily. He tried to ignore her, which was difficult for her perfume alone.

"You do know that the thing with the homework was nothing but a silly joke, don't you?"

Yes, he knew it. Still it had hurt him. He turned his head to her and tried to search for a sign in her face whether she just pretended to be nice to him and was up to more mischief ultimately. It was difficult for him to read her.

"It did not slip my attention that it was silly!", he replied harshly.

She nudged him with the elbow. "Don't take it all so serious!", she said. "Most of it is meant to be fun."

"Most of it? And how is one to know when it isn't fun for once?" If she had a reasonable answer to this question, maybe he would take her seriously, he thought to himself and looked at her avid for an answer. But she simply returned his gaze and left it to him to go on speaking.

"Moreover the question is for whom it is fun", he continued combatively.

"For both sides?" Her question sounded more like a declarative statement. Why did she talk to him in the first place, he wondered. To impress him with this nonsense? Did this girl have no sense for the commensurateness of any situation?

"If the two of us were friends, I might perhaps join your laughter about this trick. Well, I don't mean to offend you, but we aren't friends." The last part he uttered with supreme contempt.

She scrutinised him for a moment and began to laugh out loud: "I take to you!"

She laughed and he looked at her uncomprehendingly, doubting her sanity more and more. It certainly did not surprise him that they were no friends. He turned away from her and ostentatiously took another bite of his slice of bread and chewed on it angrily.

"How do you feel about us becoming friends? Because actually I wanted to ask you if you'd come to my birthday party tonight."

The food had almost fallen from his face because of his consternation. He turned towards her again and stared at her in disbelief. This had to be another trick! Or she must have lost her marbles completely. She quizzically raised an eyebrow.

"Why is that?"

"Why not?" she countered, and he wanted to object that he knew a thousand good reasons against it, but she continued: "We're in the same class, and despite your, or maybe rather because of your quiet and reserved manner you are somehow interesting."

"Well, thank you very much! You haven't taken an interest in me for so many years. Why should you start to do that just now?" he desired to know. He no longer understood the world.

"Don't we all grow up and change? Slowly we outgrow adolescence and now we see the world with different eyes. And so we also see the people around us differently. Is that so odd?" She stood his sulkiness quite composedly.

Her argument was not devoid of logic, he had to concede. Nevertheless was it so untypical for all that he had come across in this school and from these people that his scepticism's alarm sounded in his head in an ear-piercing blast.

"You must be playing a dirty trick on me! Do you really think that I would fall for that all of a sudden after what you did to me?" He was indignant.

He could not quite believe it, but her composure started to dissolve and her face really showed gentle traces of disappointment and offence. Regardless, he stood firm.

"What do you want from me anyway?"

"As I told you already," she declared with a phoney equanimous voice, "I wanted to invite you to my party. I even understand your distrust. To all intents and purposes, I can't even blame you for that. Do you know what? I will simply explain where I live and you can still make up your mind. How's that?

He agreed hesitatingly. He was pretty much beside himself, too flabbergasted at the whole situation to really think about it rationally. Therefore he let Caroline explain the way. It would not be too difficult to find, although she lived relatively far away from him. After she had finished her explanation, she stood up and went down the stairs. Halfway down she turned around to him again to tell him once more that he should make up his mind and that he could come from seven o'clock on if he wanted to. With a few smart strides she disappeared from his field of vision and he sat alone again on the marble stairs, composureless, motionless, thoughtless.

After two minutes the bell rang announcing the end of the break and hoicked him out of his numbness. He went back to the classroom and sat down on his seat. By and by the other pupils dripped into the room, mostly in twos or threes. None of them sat down, but all their gazes shaved over that one person sitting. He thought he could read a strange curiosity in the eyes of the girls and rather antipathy and a naked disdain in those of the boys. But common to all eyes were a certain incredulity and amazement.

The teacher came in and everybody sat down. Thereupon nobody took an interest in him anymore.

Snidenesses

Snidenesses she was used to for a long time,
had endured them from the very first.
She wasn't popular, neither had she friends;
everything she owned was her self and her integrity.

Maybe there were people like her abroad,
she thought to herself and moved away
only to find herself in the middle of the night
sobbing in her bed in the dark.
Roaring she had heard drunk voices,
her neighbours through the walls:
Snidenesses about the stupid stranger next door,
and guffaw.
"In vino veritas!"

Even abroad she couldn't find anybody
who was similar and familiar to her.
Those hastily hostile to her however
were everywhere and many.

She was afraid to stay
as well as to return home.
Where was the place for her?

12

The whole day long he stood beside himself. While he was eating, he was somewhere else with his thoughts, but not at the kitchen table. While he was doing his homework, he was everywhere else with his thoughts, except at his desk. When he thought about himself, he was everywhere else. When he thought about others, for example Caroline, he was only thinking about himself. And then again he was not.

His mother came home from work at around four that day. She hadn't had a shift this short for quite some time. He was staggered. When he was through with his homework, he sat down at the kitchen table opposite her. She flipped through the newspaper, nibbled at a few slices of dry crispbread and did not seem to notice him at first. He spent that time reading the boring articles overleaf. After several minutes she put down the paper and looked at him somewhat confused.

"Oh, good that you're here. There's something I have to talk to you about," she announced, but did not continue to speak. They looked at each other wordlessly instead. He did not say anything either and returned her gaze in anticipation. All of a sudden she stood up vehemently, tidied away the bread, started to clean up the kitchen while she talked to him without looking directly at him.

"There has been less and less work in the factory for quite some time now and I have tried to sham that everything remained unaffected. I've wasted away the time until evening to conceal from you that I don't work so much anymore. I had hoped that it'd get back to normal after some time, and I've procrastinated to tell you. But for some time it's getting clearer and clearer that there won't be more work again and sooner than later our money will run short. Today's paper is the last one we'll get. I've unsubscribed it. And also in every other respect I've tried to economise as much as I could."

She paused while she rummaged for something under the sink. Suddenly she started to swear, stood up and cleaned the dishes with her bare hands.

"Blimey, we don't even have a scrub sponge anymore! I don't know what's going to happen now. I know though that you are also very frugal and very close to your school-leaving exams, but it just can't go on like that!"

She began to cry, quietly as she always did. He stood up, grabbed one of the tea towels and helped her by drying the dishes. She cried very overtly, continuing to do the washing-up and speaking amid sobs.

"I wanted to enable you to study, but the rents in this city alone are way too high. We should have moved as long as we had some money left. But now you can't change schools so easily anymore and I don't know where I could find a new job. It is too late by now for you to drop out of school and do a training. The next apprenticeships will start next spring again. I'm very sorry, but I only see one possibility, namely that you quickly hunt for a side job and help me financially, even if you have to study for your exams."

She paused washing up and stared at her tiny hands.

"I hate to trouble you for it, but think it thoroughly through, and please quickly. I don't know any other way."

She ran out of the kitchen into her bedroom. He stood there at the kitchen sink stunned, as if slain, his head empty. As a matter of routine he cleaned the remainder of the dishes, dried them up and put everything back into the cabinet. Without giving it much thought, he got changed in his room, stuffed a few things into his rucksack and left the building.

The Last Time

I walk
The sun shines on my neck
The thunderclouds drift in front of me
They show me the way
I try to divert myself
But my thoughts
Draw their circles around you
As I turn around the corner
The last lightning flashes before me
I walk on
After I've lived through a moment of rest
While I admired nature for its beauty
I pass the gate
As I hear the bell ringing far away
As it seems to me
I walk through the rows of the others
Until I reach you
I lift my arms
Point at the stone
That is lying above you
That carries your name
I open my mouth and laugh
Till the tears stifle the sounds
You found him
He caught you up
Separated you and me
But not forever
'Cause I'll follow you
But not now
There is too much left to do
Too much that remained
Too much left undone

I sag down on my knees
Say a quiet, brief prayer
In the face of Him and you
At the moment
That I want to leave you
Clouds are darkening the sun
It seems to me
That I see your face
There
With a frown of regret
With bowed head
I leave this awful place
To take care of the widow again
Who you allowed back
The last time
I had talked to you
You said
Keep an eye on my wife
I know now that my time has come
To leave this cold world
Then you had closed your eyes
And left this sadness
And this cooling-off body behind

13

When he headed out it was almost seven o'clock. It took him about an hour by bus, having to change once. A lot of people were on their ways to find amusement in this night still young. They were in a jovial mood, partially half-cut already, garrulous and boisterous. He sat in a corner, witnessed their conversations and their laughter involuntarily and asked himself what exactly he was doing. He was on his way to Caroline's party, instead of going over to the stranger. He did not have a present, but she could hardly expect one when she had invited him only today at school. Why was he on his way to Caroline, he kept on asking himself incessantly. Probably it was to a certain extent his nosiness which drove him there, but pre-eminently he could not have stayed at home. He needed distance from his mother, distance from the situation she had broken to him, from the fallacious hopes which the stranger stoked, from the conditions and the attitudes which he deemed his reality. Suddenly his whole world seemed to be turned inside out and he had to find out what his take on it was. He had to make so many grave decisions, although he did not have the time to sort out his feelings. He had become very estranged to himself during these past weeks, which made things even worse and more complicated. He had to redefine himself in the light of new truths and remain true to his pain and himself at the same time. Hence he took the bull by the horns leading him all the way to Caroline. Notwithstanding he disbelieved that the way into society was the right thing for him. He still had the alternative to withdraw at any time and return to his old path, he soothed himself. But the new as well as the old path frightened him in the meantime and that terrified him the most. He had changed. He could not deny it any longer.

The house of Caroline's parents was not far from the bus stop in one of the poshest neighbourhoods of the city. With every stride on this pricey pavement he felt more and more uncomfortable. His family hadn't been too badly off in the past because of his father's income, but he had never consorted with such spheres. He mused how he was to behave when the door was opened for him, when he confronted his classmates. He conceived what it might look like in Caroline's parental home and what a party brimming with juveniles might be like at such a place. Above all he racked his brains if it was not better for him to turn back on the spot. But where else could he go to on the other hand? At the utmost there was still the stranger, who by then he felt was too dangerous. Where was all of this going to end?

Compared to the other houses and mansions in the neighbourhood, the one in front of which he stood was one of the most beautiful for ivy had crept all over one side of it bestowing it with a touch of romance that other magnificent buildings were lacking. From outside he could already hear music making the young folk dance. He saw shadows and silhouettes through the partly coloured windows.

In front of the door he examined a cast-iron foot scraper in the shape of a dachshund fascinatedly. That is, he conjectured that this something served this purpose. Anyway, this procrastination served him to have a last internal dialogue whether he should really take this step. He made an effort and tintinnabulated the doorbell of this mansion. Now that he had come all this way and with his position in the class, he had not even a dreg to lose, he encouraged himself.

He had almost envisioned that a butler opened the door, but instead it was Caroline in person standing before him. She seemed to be flabbergasted and asked him to come in. She was friendly, though admittedly not effusive, and the reception was somewhat reserved. Of course it was bizarre, because they thought to know each other after all these years together in school and at the same time they really knew each other barely.

He was about to step up to the sill when Derek emerged behind Caroline. He was the one who had denunciated him to Mr Angerman a few weeks ago. At his sight fear pumped a dose of adrenalin through his body involuntarily and made him ready for battle. Derek pushed halfway past Caroline and looked at him disparagingly in his snooty manner.

"Oh boy, look who it isn't!" Directed towards Caroline he said, "What is he doing here?"

"You know that I invited him. Do you mind that?" She was downright confident. This seemed to impress him.

"What do you have to do with this wimp? Have you invited some homeless people from the train station too?"

He felt this punch in the gut. He should have known beforehand that it was not a good idea to come here and get involved with these people. That served him right! Or had he sought for this hiding unconsciously? Now he was already in the thick of it all.

Caroline was absolutely not amused about the fashion in which Derek spoke. She turned sour, piqued and intractable.

"I invite whoever I want to. You are drunk. Go back in. And if you don't approve of it, you are free to leave at any time."

That Caroline stood her ground against Derek was not to his liking. His neck swelled, the main artery came to the fore and he pulled himself together with greatest pains as he really began to seethe. Apparently a little storm was brewing because of him and there he was standing in front of the two feeling like a hypnotised TV spectator. Although he was involved, Derek's words bounced off him, as if they did not mean him.

"Come again? You would let me leave just like that? You'd give preference to this squirt? What do you want from him anyway? Why are you suddenly so nice to him?" Derek talked himself into a rage, but each of his questions was something that he too had been wondering about. It was apparent that jealousy began to stir in Derek, who paused for a moment, then a putative insight flared up in his eyes. "You want to be with this crank, don't you? Why do you want to be with him at all? And what about me? Do you want to fuck him, you slut?"

That was the point when Caroline lost her rag and fired back. Who would not have if one was reproached in such an incredibly impudent manner? Seemingly there was more going on between them than he had realised so far, and he didn't care. At least it became clear that Caroline had been sincere with him if she was ready to suffer such malice. In a sense he felt sorry for her, but she had chosen her company herself. Therefore this was also the point when the uninvolved spectator turned around and left the scene wordlessly and unnoticed. The fight reared up and he just strode away, unaffected and yet hurt, surprised in a good way and yet feeling betrayed, an ice block and yet a heart ablaze with pity. The two were so concerned with themselves that he did not exist for them any more in that moment. He heard their voices, which contrary to every experience and in spite of the distance growing with every of his steps became louder and more aggressive. That the gestures were becoming wilder, too, he could not see, because he simply left them behind. They did not take note that he left and he did not even look back.

He wasn't alone. His companion, the pain, was with him again. He had neglected his ally for some time, but it had never left him altogether. He did not need any other company and not the pity of any Tom, Dick or Caroline either. Probably she had merely made a noble point of saving that poor depressive bloke or wanted to make amends for taking the piss out of him in order to improve her karma. But he didn't need to be saved! He didn't want to be the good deed of a girl guide. And he didn't need to brook the slanders of a drunkard. He should not have come in the first place, and yet it was the best thing that could have happened to him, for now he knew again where he belonged.

With brisk steps he walked down the brightly lit street in this dark night. Since the bus turned around a few stops further and started for its return journey after a short pause, the bus which had brought him there came almost instantaneously and gave him a ride back to the city centre. But there he did not get onto the bus going his direction, instead he walked by foot through the neon-lit centre past faltering, bawling and shady people. The most sinister one this night was he.

Away

I accompanied you
for fear of being alone.
But your presence I loathed already,
for it was intolerable for me:
Disapproval and hostility
I sensed in every unspoken word.

Disgustedly I lingered nonetheless,
hoping I was mistaken.

Again I had to comprehend
how unwelcome I was.
I waited for the right moment
and then alone I went away.

14

After a foot march of almost three hours through the cold, dark night he arrived at his place, fresh and tired at the same time. This had given him time to think. He opened the door very gently and sneaked through the flat stealthily lest to wake his mother up under any circumstances. He tiptoed into his room, emptied his rucksack, packed up the file with his poetry and some other things that were dear to him. He reached for a notepad and wrote a few lines to his mother. On a second slip he wrote to the stranger.

He went into the bath, sprinkled a little water onto his face, then he looked musingly into the mirror, turned his head to and fro, and eyed himself as intensely as he had never done before in his life, as if he wanted to engrave his look in the mirror for ever. His face was empty, neutral. He could not read anything in it, like he normally could in others. Like the lines of the hand fade after death, every expression had faded from his face. It was a grave face.

Back in his room he took a camera out of a drawer and took pictures of himself with an arm stretched out, which no one except his mother ever saw. He shouldered his bag and put the letter to the stranger in his pocket. The letter to his mother he placed onto the kitchen table along with the camera. Without squandering another glance through the dwelling, he left the flat as soundlessly as he had entered it. A ghost at witching hour.

He walked down the street to the house of the stranger. Taking the letter out of his jacket pocket he slid it into the respective letter box. The entire house was dark. There weren't any lights on in the apartment rooms facing the entrance side, not in those of the stranger either. He rang the bell at this house immediately and without hesitation, unlike at Caroline's before. This time he was sure what he was doing—at least that's what he thought. For a long time nothing happened, not even a light went on, but then the intercom crackled and the voice of the stranger said: "Who is it?"

He leaned a bit down towards the intercom and answered with a firm voice: "I've come to bid farewell."

"It's in the middle of the night, much too late for doorbell pranks", it rustled through the speaker, then it crackled again and the intercom was silent.

Presumably he had jolted the stranger from sleep, so that groggily he had not discerned who it was. Probably it was better this way and irrelevant now. The other one would find his letter in the morning and understand.

He turned around, looked down the street and deeply breathed in the odourless autumn air. The time had come! He placed one foot in front of the other and every footfall carried him deeper into the woods and farther away from the humans. The forest was gloomy and as eerie as ever. Still he didn't feel queasy, uneasy, when he heard the call of an owl or a cracking in the thicket. A shiver ran down his spine thereupon, but this was an involuntary reaction of his body, nothing more. His soul however was calm and composed, for it knew that nothing and no one could prevent it from reaching its aim this time and going back to the place it called home.

After a good distance the trees stepped aside and opened the view to the hillock on which his old friend, the oak, stood wrapped in the wan light of the moon. It was denuded now, for autumn had finally snatched its foliage frock in passing. At its shadowy sight he felt mirth and confidence, but also compassion for his mother. He wanted to lift his burden from her. On his way up to the oak his eyes filled with tears, tears rife with disconsolate grief and unhealed anguish, tears rife with rejoicing and happiness of completion. On his ultimate path all his soul's stirrings arose from their deep grave and refilled his body, which had been devoid for so long.

Coming closer he saw how the perfect noose was still hanging from the boughs of the tree, its only emblazonment. As before he put his rucksack down at the roots of his friend leaning it against its trunk, but this time he did it consciously and purposely. He climbed into the crown, his fast end in view.

The rope was damp and cold and as a result tighter. He tenderly stroked the grey coarse braiding with his left hand. He sat down on the limb on which he had been perching, his legs dangling over the deep ground. With both hands he grasped the loop of the noose, pulled it over his head and tightened it around his neck. It scraped over his face and his neck.

He took a deep last breath, self-aware, as if he wanted to suck in the whole world. He felt a tickling on his shoulder, then something like a touch. There it was again, the phantom touch. He looked around, but he did not find anything in the darkness. Nothing but his pain was with him. No stranger, no angel. Once again his gaze glided over the landscape and over to the moon, which twinkled behind the last clouds. He closed his eyes and the sickle was the last thing branding itself onto his retina. Staring in the face of death he was as sober and self-conscious as never before in his life. He perceived everything as real as never before. If he hadn't really lived consciously, then at least he wanted to die all the more consciously.

He let himself glide forward. After a short fall colours and stars exploded in his mind's eye...

Life is Pain

My life is amiss and ill,
so that I drown in its flood.
It's need I cannot fulfil.
Am I too good of blood?

I don't want to bear it
to be ill-fated and starred.
But I neither despair it
that my lot is so hard.

Agony and loss are life
the way I perceive.
Survival's my strife,
forfeiture bore grief.

To others I'm an annoyance,
But soon I'll bring them deliverance.

15

I shuffled back into the bedroom. Somebody had woken me up in the middle of the night. I was about to go back to sleep when my head was abruptly, dumbfoundedly sober and I realised who the one at the door had been and what he had been saying. I understood at last. Rushing I put on some clothes, searched for a torch and ran out of the house as swiftly as I could. Long I wandered around on my search until the idea struck me that I might find him at the oak on the hill.

When Ellie and I arrived there, it was already too late. It was a horrible sight, but also a tranquil one. He hung calmly with his back towards me in the crown of the naked oak, clearly visible even from a distance. I made no attempts to get him down, I only took his backpack with his treasure, which stood at the foot of the tree, like a finder's reward, and went back to my place. On my way I was having strong pangs of remorse at first, because I had not reacted quickly enough, later my feelings of guilt were eased by the certainty that he had chosen this consciously. It surely would have been impossible to dissuade him from his plan.

Back at home I did not call the police immediately but waited until the early morning. Until then I killed the time, in which it would have been impossible for me to sleep, by read Wulf's poems and stories page by page. They were a peculiar jumble of feelings, impressions, contradictions. The observant reader might not have failed to notice that I have used some of his poems here to accentuate his moods with his words.

Around six o'clock, when I had read most of it, I picked up the phone and informed the police. Ten minutes later the constabulary picked me up, so that I showed them the way, and we drove along the forest path in the police car. An emergency ambulance followed us. It was weird to go this route by car and without Ellie. I stared out of the window, tired and dopey, while the trees were breezing along. Their boles, aflame in the blue light originating from the vehicles, sparked a strange mood in me, although it wasn't that alone.

The dangling silhouette was visible from afar at the crack of dawn. I stayed inside the police car, yawning, angry, weeping, and observed how the officers searched the scene for traces that they could not find. There was only a rope and a body. The evidence was authoritative: self-inflicted death. I concealed the bag with the poems, because they were irrelevant for the police. They would not have understood them anyway.

When they had lifted the body down and searched it, they found his wallet with his identity card, so that his identity was disclosed at last. Until this point in time I had not known his last name. They announced his name over the radio and informed his mother, who went straight away to the morgue where the corpse was brought anon. My personal details were taken down for potential questions later, then they dropped me off at the street corner near my house.

I entered the house and only at that time did I find his farewell note. I hasted up to my flat, put the kettle on for tea and provided for Ellie doddering through the room. Not until I had a strong tea in my hand did I muster the courage to read the letter.

Roman,

I like you and that is my dilemma. Because even if we might become friends eventually, this must not be, for I should not be alive and probably won't when you read this!

I am sorry that I have dragged you into this in the last weeks and that I must hurt you now! That's how everybody close to me fared, which is why I stayed away from the world. Unfortunately you were nothing but a slip in this respect. Forgive me!

In fact I am dead already for many a long year, but I had cheated my fate and had wrested a few more years from it with false dice. But at what price? And what's the use of it now?

I live and yet my life is worth nothing. It is totally unenjoyable. I live in constant remorse and guilt, a life guilt for a death guilt. I cannot bear this burden any longer. Stale is the triumph of life; therefore I return the stolen goods by my own choice. I give my life to redeem the guilt and annihilate the pain.

We are made from ash and dust, so I go back to the Earth. But in case we are children of the stars, I'll return thither.

Fare well!

16

I spoke to his mother only once after his funeral. She told me about the car accident in which both his father and his twin brother had lost their lives. The parents had divided a list of tasks and, as usual, each of them had taken a son, only this one time not according to the rotation. She told me that it had been a spontaneous idea of her husband not to take along Wulf, whose turn it was, but his brother Rhys instead, so that Wulf went with his mother for another errand before the whole family was to go on vacation. She also told me about the financial situation and her appeal to her son. She blamed herself to have lost her whole family and failed as a mother. I wanted to give her the file of poems, but she told me that as Wulf's only friend I should keep it. She even gave me a few pictures of him.

All the teachers and pupils of his class attended the burial, some other people too, but his mother must have noticed very quickly that none of them truly mourned for her son. All of them were wearing pitiful, dishonestly afflicted faces, but none revealed the depth of amicable loss.

The town, virtually the whole country, was in uproar in the days and weeks after this incident. The media reported on this case. Politicians and the population, parents and the teachers' union were galvanised and discussed, lamented and pointed fingers. The media were responsible, because they glorified violence and conveyed the wrong values. At one point the teachers were blamed, who were not trained enough psychologically, then again the parents—though this was only dared to be expressed as a generalization, because nobody wanted to reproach this poor single mother who had done everything for her son. The films he had watched were blamed, the music he had listened to. Only

Shakespeare almost escaped the blame, because he was a classic—although some few pert voices did also allocate a part of the guilt to his depressed Hamlet.

But deep in their hearts no one understood him verily. Nobody really wanted to understand him, for dealing with this matter would have posed too many obscure points and unsolvable riddles. For everybody else, except his mother and me, this was only another incident of the tragic decline in values which served as a subject of discussion for some time. Afterwards the own illnesses or the weather had to be moaned about again. The truth of life written in his story didn't mean anything to anybody. He, the human being, did not matter to them.

To me his mother spoke about quite many a thing, with the reporters she did not want to talk. She did not want her wounds to be torn open even more. She told me, her son's only friend as it turned out—rather an acquaintance, but I hid this from her—, that she had repressed the loss of her husband and her first son, she even had had to repress it to be able to carry on, to function, in order to feed her other son. She elegised how difficult it had been to work after the death of her beloved ones, because she had been full of sorrow, because she had not learned a trade and had to do cheap and laborious work. She bewailed the difficulty of slogging away so that her son had a little something and having to watch how he withdrew more and more, locking himself away, turning cold and indifferent. She had convinced herself privily to believe that he was happy and had many friends, which was why he spent so little time at home. She rued that she had not been able to care more about him, because she had to hustle.

Even if she did not speak about it openly, I could read in her eyes filled with shame and reddened by tears that Wulf had not been her darling. She had been forced to repress and sublimate her fury that he had lived in Rhys's stead through the furious industriousness for Wulf's well-being. She was not aware of it and I definitely didn't hold it against her, but this repressed ire must surely have been what in turn had made her indifferent to Wulf's withdrawal.

After the funeral I never saw her again. A few days later it was making headlines that she had passed away with grief at having outlived her whole family, which fuelled the national interest and discussion. I have heard rumours in the neighbourhood that it had been an overdose of pills.

Wulf must have entertained very conflicting feelings throughout his youth. On the one hand he was mad at his father that he had left him in the lurch and had ultimately chosen his brother; on the other hand he owed him his life. In addition he mourned his brother, who strangely enough had been given preference by many people, as I had read between the lines. The question what it was about him that wasn't equally good must have nagged at Wulf persistently. His feelings for his mother had seemingly been inconsistent as well, for on the one hand she had done everything in her power, if only after he was the only one she had left, but on the other hand he knew too well that he was but the only one, yet not the dearest one. And into the bargain he carried the heavy burden of a life and survival guilt which he felt because he lived in his brother's stead. This was why he hated his life the most.

Probably nobody will ever be able to paint the whole picture of Wulf. Even the few tesserae that I could assemble do not even allow us to sneak a peek on his true shadow. Who is capable of fully comprehending a person at large? Who can comprehend themselves entirely?

The more I have concerned myself with Wulf, the better I understand him. But what is more important is that through him I understand myself a great deal better, that I feel my will to live even more strongly. He too had a strong will to live, but his guilt, his loneliness and his death drive prevailed finally. His death had been a conscious decision. Because of him I now live much more consciously. I live through him, for him, and especially I live for myself. His brother died for him. He died for his brother. I however choose life for him.

Go On

A year could not change
that you are gone
Every night I'd like to help you
find your new path,
for I know that my
mourning binds your soul.

Just go on!
It is about time!
Don't stay behind
because of our tears!

Please go on!
Your life beyond
remembrance waits for you.
Go on!
Someday we will meet again
and we will see:
Everything was fine that way.
Therefore, do go on!